DARK WARNING

Marie-Louise Fitzpatrick

Orion
Children's Books

First published in Great Britain in 2012
by Orion Children's Books
a division of the Orion Publishing Group Ltd
Orion House
5 Upper St Martin's Lane
London WC2H 9EA
A Hachette UK Company

1 3 5 7 9 10 8 6 4 2

A catalogue record for this book is available
from the British Library.

Trade Paperback ISBN 978 1 84255 678 8
Hardback ISBN 978 1 4440 0191 4

Typeset by Input Data Services Ltd, Bridgwater, Somerset

Printed and bound by CPI Group (UK) Ltd, Croydon, CR0 4YY

The Orion Publishing Group's policy is to use
papers that are natural, renewable and recyclable products
made from wood grown in sustainable forests. The logging
and manufacturing processes are expected to conform to
the environmental regulations of the country of origin.

www.orionbooks.co.uk

DARK
WARNING

Also by Marie-Louise Fitzpatrick

Timecatcher

To the memory of my darling gran, Dote O' Neill, who told me many, many stories, including that of Billy.

1

I was about four when I saw Matt Davern's spaniel bite John Reilly's hand. Nothing strange in that 'cept I saw that dog bite John Reilly a full five minutes before John Reilly even reached out to pat the cross old thing.

'I saw,' I said to Da as we went home later, me high on his shoulders looking down at all the world.

'Saw what, lovey?' Da smiled up at me as we wended between the carts and stalls of Smithfield Market towards Missus Kenny's lodging house.

'Saw Matt Davern's spaniel bite John Reilly,' I replied, watching feathers float by on passing hats and women hitching their long petticoats to stop them sweeping the dirty cobbles.

'Sure an' we all saw that, Taney girl.' Da laughed. 'And half o' Dublin heard John Reilly roar!'

'But I saw it two times, Da,' I said proudly.

Da stopped walking. 'What d'you mean, lovey?' His voice was slow and careful. 'What d'you mean, Taney?' he asked again.

'Saw the dog bite John Reilly before it bited him,' I said, a little unsure of myself now.

'I see,' Da said.

'Have I been bad, Da?' I could feel my lower lip quivering. Da's voice was strange, not like Da's at all.

I tried to peer around his head to see his face and he patted my leg. 'No, lovey, you haven't been bad.' He began to walk again and I had to lean back and hold on. 'You'll tell me any time that happens, won't you, Taney?'

I told him I would. I promised.

It didn't happen again till when I was maybe six or thereabouts. We were in the market and Da was haggling with a trader over a bushel of carrots. I pulled at his coat tails to get his attention.

'Jenna Mooney's going to tear her petticoat and make the fish fall about,' I said, pointing at the small yellow-haired girl running through the stalls.

The root seller raised his eyebrows and Da half-smiled. We three watched the girl run past the long row of milking cows, the cabbage man, the costermonger and the orange seller. As she passed the fishmonger the tail of her brown petticoat snagged on the broken reeds of a battered basket. She yanked herself free and the basket spun out from the display causing more baskets to tilt and lots of fish to flop and slap onto the cobbles. The fishmonger swore and Jenna Mooney took one look at what she'd done and scarpered down Duck Lane.

I giggled and looked up at Da. His face had turned pale.

'Well, I'll be . . .' the root man was saying, laughing loudly as he watched the monger slide about in his wares, trying to set things to rights. 'An' how did yer young one make that happen, then?'

'She didn't,' Da snapped, grabbing my hand and moving us away from the stall.

'Da?' I said, running to keep up with his long strides. 'Please, Da, you're going too fast an' you're hurting me hand.'

He slowed down but didn't look at me.

'D-Da?' I began to whimper.

He stopped then, knelt down and pulled me into his arms. I sobbed into his shoulder. 'I didn't make it happen, Da,' I hiccupped. 'I just saw it in me head, Da. I just saw it and then it happened, I swear.'

He nodded and smiled but the smile didn't reach his eyes.

'Couldn't help it, Da,' I said.

He nodded again. 'I know, lovey.' He stood up and tossed my curly hair with his big hand. 'I'd just rather ...' He sighed. 'It doesn't matter. Forget about it, lovey.'

But I couldn't forget the look on Da's face that day. So when I knew Mick Bryson would slip in dung in Thundercut Alley a whole day before it happened, I didn't tell Da. I felt awful afterwards 'cause Mick Bryson hurt his ankle so bad he couldn't work for a month and I could have stopped him comin' a cropper if I'd only said what I'd seen.

I never said when I knew Missus Mooney's new baby was going to get took by measles, and it would have made no differ if I had.

I never said anything the time I knew a horse would go crazy in the square and knock hawkers and gawkers and stalls about before trying to jump over the milk cart and breaking its front legs. I never said nowt, but I made sure I wasn't about that day to hear its screams.

3

I never said nowt and eventually Da stopped watching me with a worried frown on his face. And he stopped asking if I ever saw anything strange, like that time I'd seen Matt Davern's spaniel bite John Reilly's hand.

It was the Misses Davies who told me about my mother. My mother was dead and gone and me only a baby, so I couldn't remember her. Da never talked about her, not to me. The two Misses Davies often did; that's why I liked to go downstairs to visit with them. That, and their rooms smelled of lavender and rose water while most of the world smelled of boiled cabbage and sweat.

The Misses Davies had the best rooms in Missus Kenny's house, the whole floor above the shop, with the front rooms facing out onto Smithfield Square. Their rooms were full of lovely things and never hung about with wet clothes like ours were. There was a handsome sofa with curly arms and legs, and some upright chairs, three little walnut tables all tucked one inside the other, and a dresser full of fancy silver dishes and little porcelain statues of milkmaids and shepherds. More bits and pieces than you could shake a stick at, there was.

No one else in our lodging house owned much; near all of the furniture in every other room belonged to Missus Kenny. The Misses Davies were old ladies, as much as fifty year old even, but they were elegant and fine. They always had lace at their throats and wrists and their hair caught up with many clips and pins. They were the grandest ladies I knew. They drank tea on Friday afternoons and would invite me to join them. They were fond of company, the Misses Davies, but

4

they didn't seem to know many folk so they made do with Missus Kenny and me.

I liked to look at the beautiful things in the Misses Davies' rooms, to sit on the embroidered footstool, to rub my bare feet in the Turkish rug, and take tea from a china cup. Tea! We never had tea, me and Da and Mary Kate and Jon Jon. I wasn't sure I really liked the taste of it but Miss Evelyn let me put lots of honey in.

'Your mother was a true beauty,' the two Misses Davies would say. 'All that lovely red hair, just like yours.'

'And those extraordinary grey eyes,' Miss Evelyn Davies would say in her posh voice. 'Like autumn clouds.'

'You have your mother's eyes,' Miss Ruth would add. 'Though yours are slightly paler and larger, I think.'

'Your mother's eyes,' they'd say again, glancing at each other. Then they'd stare at me, like they wanted to ask something but weren't sure iffen they should. Sometimes Miss Ruth would clear her throat and start to speak but Miss Evelyn would frown slightly and that'd be that.

'Go on, then, ask me,' I said one day when I couldn't stand it no longer. 'I don't mind, whatever it is. Ask.'

Miss Evelyn slopped her tea as she put the cup back into the saucer, and Miss Ruth hid her mouth behind her handkerchief.

'Can it be?' Miss Ruth whispered. 'Has she read our thoughts? Has she . . . has she——?'

'Got her dear mama's gift?' Miss Evelyn clutched at her sister's arm.

'My mother had a gift?' I frowned. 'What d'you mean?'

'Your mama had a gift, a talent,' Miss Evelyn explained. 'Some people are born to paint wonderful pictures; some naturally have splendid singing voices. Your mother – well – she had a rather unusual talent.' She looked quickly at her sister. 'But maybe we shouldn't speak of this.'

'Please, Miss Evelyn,' I begged, anxious not to lose this chance to learn more about my mother. By now my face must have looked all question, just like theirs. Even Horace, the Misses Davies' grumpy old cat, looked kind of curious. 'She was my mam,' I said, digging my dirty toes into the carpet, my fingers into the cushion I was sat on. 'I have a right to know about her, I do.'

Miss Evelyn put a finger to her lips and Miss Ruth took the lace hankie away from hers.

'Evelyn,' she began. 'Don't you think perhaps . . .'

'Perhaps.'

'Perhaps?'

'Yes.'

'We should?' Miss Ruth said, uncertain.

'Yes.' Miss Evelyn nodded and they both put their hands into their laps.

By now I wanted to shout at them, 'Tell me, tell me!' but I held my tongue for fear they'd change their minds and not tell me at all. I suddenly knew just what they were going to say but I needed to hear them say it out loud.

'Your mother,' Miss Evelyn began. 'Your mother, she—'

'Your mother saw things before they happened,' Miss Ruth blurted out, then drew her hankie over her mouth again.

'She had the gift of second sight,' Miss Evelyn said. 'She

knew things about people, accidents that might befall them, good fortune that might be on its way.'

'Whether their next child would be a girl or a boy.'

'When they might meet their true love.' They both giggled and two hankies fluttered. 'She read our tea leaves for us every month.'

'Read your tea leaves?' I'd never heard of such a thing.

'We would pour ourselves a cup of tea, then drink it,' Miss Ruth explained eagerly, picking up her cup as she spoke.

'Then Ella, your mama, would look at the pattern that the leaves left in the cup,' Miss Evelyn said, 'and tell us what she saw in store for us there. Trifles, mainly. When Horace was just a kitten she said he'd go missing for a day or so but all would be well and he would return. And once when Ruth lost a pearl earring, Ella said it was fallen between the floorboards. And she could always foretell when we should expect a visit from an old friend.'

'And,' Miss Ruth lifted her cup to her lips and drained it, 'she was always right.'

'Always.' Miss Evelyn nodded and drank her tea.

They put down their cups and slid them towards me across the table. I looked at the mess of leaves in the little bowls.

Horace will have a fight with the biggest of the distillery cats, I thought. He'll lose a piece of his ear and get real sick. I drew my head back. I thought of Da's face that day in the market when I'd said that Jenna Mooney'd knock over the fish baskets.

'I can't do it,' I said, and shook my head. 'Tea leaves is just tea leaves to me.'

Their faces fell. They looked so disappointed I almost took it back. But what was the use of telling them about Horace? There's no stopping a cat fighting when it chooses.

'Never mind, my dear,' Miss Evelyn said, withdrawing her cup and smiling. 'It was so entertaining whenever your mother consented to read our leaves for us but I think her gifts weighed heavy on her in the end.'

Miss Ruth nodded her head and sighed. 'Perhaps you shouldn't mention to your father that we told you?' The two ladies looked at me anxiously.

I assured them I wouldn't say a word, but I got them to tell me more about my mother's gift every time I came to call. I never tired of hearing the Misses Davies say how my hair was just like my mam's and how my eyes were near as grey. I never tired of hearing how she'd read their cups and how she'd seen things that hadn't happened yet. Second sight, they called it; I had a name for it now.

I went on hiding it from me da but I stopped trying to push it away. I stopped thinking it was bad now I knew it came from my mother. As I got older I began to hear whispers from other folk about Ella Tyrell's gift. It seems some folk blamed her for it and some admired her for it, but I don't suppose she could help it either way.

And me. I couldn't help it neither.

2

Horace got his ear bit the very next week. A great lump was tore out of it and he near died from the fever that came on him. The Misses Davies cried and fussed till Missus Kenny found them a woman in the market who knew which herbs to use. He healed up at last and the old ladies spoilt him so much that he grew too fat to ever go fighting the distillery cats again.

'Them ladies an' that cat.' Missus Kenny rolled her eyes. 'An' it as bad-tempered as a badger.'

Missus Kenny thought I looked like my mother too, though she wasn't as polite about it as the Misses Davies.

'Yer the spit of yer mam, Taney Tyrell,' she'd bawl. ''Tis a wonder o' nature how you can look so like her an' still be as plain as plain can be. Ella Tyrell used turn the head o' every man that ever see'd her, so she did, but she never had eyes for anyone but yer da.'

Missus Kenny owned our lodging house. She ran the shop downstairs and lived in the rooms behind it. It was a second-hand clothes shop, full to the door and beyond with clothes of every sort, except new. If you were in the know, she might sell you some goods from down below in the cellar, mostly illegal second-hand tea leaves that had been used once already in a rich man's parlour. Servants would collect them up and dry them, then sell their month's gatherings to Missus Kenny for a penny. She'd bulk it up with some dried nettles and sell it on the sly for a third the price of brand new tea.

There were other things down that cellar that she wasn't supposed to have, things she hadn't paid the proper taxes on – foreign spirits, salt, soap, coffee. She'd say, with a wink, that she'd no idea how they got there and that she had better get rid of them quick, before the excise man came calling.

We lived up top of the house, me, Da, Mary Kate and Jon Jon. It was an old fashioned Dutch Billy house, brick-built. It had a flat front to it, plain all the way to the top, where it formed into two big curves with a window in the middle of each and a dip in between them. The curved pediments hid two red roof gables. We lived in one gable; a student called Edward Manning had the other.

Ed Manning wrote verse, so he took to calling his room his 'poet's sky parlour'. Mary Kate said that was just silly, that an attic was an attic and calling it a fancy name wouldn't make the room any less poky nor the ceiling any less sloped. But I understood why Ed Manning did it. Down on the street all was muck and dust and dung, noise and hustle and throng. Up in our gable the city's noise fell away a little, even the bawling of the street criers was no more irritating than the calling of passing seagulls. From our window we could see Smithfield Market Square below. It was called a square even though it was about five times as long as it was wide. Our house was on the long west side, opposite Jameson's Distillery;

we could see clean into the yard. If I opened the window and leaned out as far as I could, I was able to see the other end of the market. On good days, I could even see the Dublin Mountains far away. Sometimes, when Mary Kate had been telling me off or I was feeling lonely, I'd think: iffen I could just fly, I'd fly to them mountains. Fly away with the birds.

There was a table in our room and some stools, a dresser and a window seat that doubled as my bed. Over at one wall there was a straw mattress Da and Mary Kate slept on. We were lucky to have a fireplace in the corner. The wood had to be carried up all them stairs but Da was big and strong and he made light of hoisting bundles of logs from the backyard.

Me da's name was Milo. He was tall, taller than most any man in Stoneybatter, Smithfield and all of Dublin city, so, of course, everyone called him Miles-high Tyrell. On market days you could see him clear above the crowd, even if he was across the square and five hundred people and three hundred cattle stood 'tween you and him.

'Yer da's cruel tall,' Missus Kenny would say, cackling loudly, making all her chins wobble and her long earrings swing. 'Cruel tall and wicked handsome.'

When the Misses Davies spoke of Da they'd smile wistfully and shake their grey heads in unison.

'Poor Mister Tyrell,' they'd say. 'He adored your mother. The light quite went out of his eyes when she passed away.'

'They made such a handsome couple,' Miss Ruth would add with a sigh.

'Of course your stepmother is a very good sort of woman,'

Miss Evelyn would quickly interrupt. 'Your father has found much happiness again, we're sure.'

Da married Mary Kate when I was five. She was a countrywoman, robust and red-cheeked. When she first came to live with us in our little attic room she was kind enough and would cuddle me and call me Taney love, and Taney pet. She taught me my letters, though it was the Misses Davies that taught me to read and write proper. Mary Kate was proud that I could read when most of the kids about us had no schooling at all, but by the time I was eight she had me down as lazy and a dreamer, and in a few more years she was calling me useless and selfish and spoilt. By then she'd had Jon Jon. My da and me loved Jon Jon just as well as she did but Mary Kate seemed set on keeping the best of his love all to herself.

'Leave him be, he's sleepin',' she'd say when I tried to help with him.

'Leave him be, you're squeezin' him.'

'Leave him be. Sure and you're spillin' more food then he's atin'. Sweep the floor if you've nowt to be doin'.'

But I didn't want to sweep the floor; I wanted to play with my sweet baby brother. Seen as Mary Kate wouldn't let me do as I wanted, it was out the door with me and down the stairs. Missus Kenny and the Misses Davies used the front door that opened onto the square; us in the gables used the side door that led into Thundercut Alley. I'd stop a minute to choose where I would spend my day – down by the river, or round about the lanes, or on the big green behind Queen Street, or further off in the fields and boreens where Stoneybatter ended and the countryside began.

I think Mary Kate was secretly happy to see the back of me and have the room and Jon Jon to herself, but it went hard with her to see me spend my days wandering and dreaming and picking flowers in ditches.

'She does nothin' to help,' she grumbled to Da one evening, as he ate his dinner.

Da gave a grunt that could have meant anything and went on eating.

'And if she does, she does it so ill I have to do it all over again, and what use is that, I ask you?'

'Girl's only young yet,' Da said. 'Let her have her freedom another wee while.'

Mary Kate went all prim. 'The devil makes work for idle hands,' she said with a sniff. 'She'll turn out like her mother yet.'

Da stopped the knife halfway to his mouth and his eyes clouded over. He turned to me and searched my face, like he was looking for something there and hoping he wouldn't find it. I knew what it was he was looking for now, but I tried not to let it show.

'You need to start doin' yer bit about the house, Taney girl,' he said. 'A bit o' work and you can be off playin' as you choose.'

And then he was watching me again, watching with fear in the corner of his eye. And, for a while, I tried my best to help Mary Kate. Then Da forgot to watch me and I forgot to help out and went back to running around the streets and lanes just like before.

3

One morning when I was maybe eleven year old I woke up knowing certain-sure that trouble was coming to Missus Kenny's door. I didn't stop to think; I was down the stairs like lightning. It was only when Missus Kenny was standing there, bleary in her night shift, asking me what in the name of all that was holy I thought I was about, bangin' on her door an' it not even light yet, that I realised I was going to give myself away good and proper.

'The excise man is comin', Missus Kenny, ma'am,' I mumbled.

'Lord God Almighty, child! The excise man!' Missus Kenny turned quite white and grabbed the door jamb for support. 'Did you see him from the attic window or what?'

'Yes.' I lied quickly. 'I seen him from the window.'

Missus Kenny shoved me out of the way and squinted across the square. The first herd of cattle was lumbering in, there were a few horses hauling carts of hay and some market people setting up their stalls and huts, but no one that could be the excise man.

'Are you makin' fun of me, you little rossie?' Missus Kenny

rounded on me, ready to box my ears. 'You heard me tell yer da the other night that I was afeard the excise man would come an' find that fine keg o' brandy I got wrong side o' the law an' you decided you'd play a trick on old Missus Kenny, is that it?' She'd turned purple, angry fit to burst.

'He *is* coming, Missus Kenny, I swear, and he's got two watchmen with him.' I looked over my shoulder nervously, caught now between the trouble coming for Missus Kenny and the trouble I was bringing on myself. 'Please, Missus Kenny, I think I dreamed it, Missus Kenny, but you've got to hide that brandy all the same.'

She breathed in sharp and leaned back to take a better look at my face. 'Dreamed it, did you?' She raised her eyebrows, considering me long and hard, then pulled her keys from within the folds of her nightdress and grabbed her shawl from behind the door. 'Get yer da,' she said. 'I'll be needin' help movin' that brandy keg an' the sacks o' tea.'

'No, please, not me da, me da mustn't know I told you,' I stuttered. 'Please, Missus.'

Missus Kenny was already halfway down the stairs to the cellar. She waggled her free hand back up at me. 'All right. We'll tell yer da I got a tip-off from someone in the know. Now fetch him, quick.'

The excise man came an hour later. He turned the shop and cellar inside out but found nothing there that wasn't bought legal and proper. When he was gone Missus Kenny hauled herself up the backstairs and tapped on our door, panting and puffing. Da was off at work by then; it was just me and Mary Kate and Jon Jon. I was teaching Jon Jon to walk, holding his wee hands and he wobbling and chuckling all the way across the room.

Missus Kenny beamed at me as she came in the door and held out a paper cone of tea to Mary Kate. 'Saved me a whole heap o' trouble, the young one did,' she said. 'A fat fine at least, maybe even a gaol sentence. That's just a little token of me appreciation.'

I squeezed Jon Jon's hands so tight he yelped. I shook my head desperately at Missus Kenny but she didn't pay any heed.

Mary Kate's brow creased into a puzzled frown. 'What did Taney do?' she said. 'I don't understand, ma'am.'

'Oh, now!' Missus Kenny chortled and pushed Mary Kate's shoulder playfully. 'I understand it's to be a secret an' Jane Kenny can keep a secret with the best o' them. I always said girl's spit of her mam. Seems she got more than her mammy's red hair, eh? An' a good thing for me she did, an' all.'

Mary Kate shot me a look that'd kill a horse. 'I'm not sure what you mean, Missus Kenny,' she said stiffly.

'Oh, me lips is sealed, dearie. Like the grave, I am. No one will hear it from me.' Missus Kenny patted Mary Kate's arm. 'But 'tis awful good to know there's someone amongst us what can see trouble comin' an' give a poor soul some warnin', that's all I'll say.' She pressed the tea into Mary Kate's hand. 'She says her da is not to know. I suppose he doesn't like to be minded of Ella, the creature? Ella's gift was a trouble to her, I know, so we'll say nothin' to him, but 'tween us women we can speak plain. Taney has the second sight, just like her mam, God rest her soul. An' today Jane Kenny has good reason to thank the Lord for it.'

'Thank the Lord for it indeed,' Mary Kate hissed when our landlady was gone. She dropped the cone of tea on the floor as if it burned her to touch a reward earned in such a wicked way. 'What has He got to do with it, I ask you?'

She crossed herself and grabbed a bottle of holy well water from the shelf. She began to toss it around the room, over me, over Jon Jon. She near emptied the whole thing, as if she'd wash the entire room in it if she could, and me and Jon Jon too. When she was done, she turned on me. She grabbed my arms and shook me hard.

'I'll not have yer mother's witchery in my home, Taney Tyrell. No good can come o' such things.' She shook me again for emphasis. 'I'll not tell yer da, not this time. But you'll never do that or anythin' like it again, you hear?'

I nodded miserably, my teeth chattering and tears rolling down my cheeks. I think Mary Kate would have shook me for ever if Jon Jon hadn't started to roar. She let me go and went to comfort him. I stumbled to the door to make my escape and didn't come back till bedtime.

Mary Kate was as good as her word; she didn't tell Da what I had done but she watched me like a hawk, she set me errands to keep me busy, and she chided me for every small thing ill-done. She'd hardly let me hold Jon Jon for fear I'd taint him with my badness. She seemed determined to beat me mam's gift out of me, if it was the last thing she ever did.

But she drank Missus Kenny's tea all the same.

4

I never really fitted easy with the other children round about but I played with the Mooney kids sometimes – yellow-haired Jenna and Jimmy and Finn.

The Mooneys lived out back in the yard, all eight of them squashed in a little shack behind the lodging house, beside the stable where Slow Hannah, Missus Kenny's old horse, lived. Mary Kate didn't like the Mooneys much; I sometimes played with them just to get up her nose.

We went down to the gravel slip that day because it was hot and the boys wanted to swim. The quays were still being built alongside the river, forcing it to run narrower all the way from the Bloody Bridge to Dublin Bay. Back at the Royal Barracks the river was much wider. A big circle of gravel sloped down to the water's edge. Me and Jenna could only paddle but the boys stripped off and jumped in. I envied them. All that fresh water, cleaning their skin and hair. Not that them boys cared about that. They were all about the splashing and the yelling and showing off how long they could hold their breath under water.

I hitched up my petticoat and paddled my feet, washed my hands right up to the elbows and rubbed my face and neck.

A luxury, it was, and one I wouldn't have much longer now I had turned thirteen – near grown up. The Quality liked to take the air along the Gravel Walk and we weren't really supposed to bathe ourselves here, but so long as we were kids we could disguise it as playing. I sat down on the stones beside Jenna and watched the lads as they larked about, pushing each other down and laughing.

Suddenly outta nowhere I began to feel queasy. I lay back on the gravel. To distract myself from the awful spinning sensation inside my head I closed my eyes and tried to imagine what it would be like to be in the river.

The water will be icy-cold on my skin, I thought, and I'll hold my breath and put my head under the surface so as I'm whole and entire in the water. My hair will spread out around me and my scalp'll tingle as the river flows over my head. I stretch my arms to either side and float; the river is flowing all about me and I'm flowing with it.

The Liffey is gurgling and singing. It sings of mountains and bog, grasses and flowers, otters and birds. It sings of feathers and scales flashing and flickering. It sings of tiny flying, hopping, skipping, buzzing things. It sings life; it sings death. It sings in peat browns and rusty oranges, gold-green and olive. It sings wild grey and sparkling blue; it sings of the sea. The Liffey sings and I sing with it; me and the river sing as we flow to the bay. I've never felt anything like the joy I feel at this moment. I want to stay here for ever, forever flowing to the sea, but someone is shouting my name, screaming it over and over, so I open my eyes.

I haven't imagined any of it. I'm in the water, under it,

inside it. I must have walked into it with my eyes shut like a sleepwalker. I look below and see stones and broken barrels, and green stuff growing and twirling around my dangling legs. I look up, and the bridge and the buildings and the sky waggle about above the surface of the water.

Didn't know I could swim, I think lazily.

I rise to the surface and hear the screaming again. Jenna Mooney screeching my name.

'I'm here,' I call, but she's huddled over something on the gravel slip, pushing it frantically with her hands. Finn and Jimmy are wading out of the water to her side. What's she saying?

'Taney's dead, Taney's dead.'

I laugh at her silliness but I suppose I should go over and see what she's going on about just the same. Reluctantly I leave the water. Up, up, I rise, air rushing around me, then down, down to where Jenna and her brothers crouch.

'Taney's dead, I tell you,' I hear her wail. Her brothers and me, we look over Jenna's shoulder.

And there I am, still and white, lying on the gravel.

Finn pokes me with his toe. 'Jays,' he says, face creased in horror. 'What'll we tell her da? He'll kill us, he will.'

I stare at myself. I'm lying there on the slip and I'm here floating in the air above it. How can that be? Jenna begins to bawl. Jimmy lifts the me lying on the gravel by the shoulders.

'Wake up, Taney,' he yells, right into my face. 'Wake up.'

I look once more at the river and it calls to me. The sea, the sea, it seems to be saying.

I turn back to the body on the gravel. Next moment, I'm back inside it, sitting up and coughing.

'Thanks be to God,' Finn says, blessing himself.

'We thought you were d-dead,' Jenna sobs, throwing her arms around my neck.

It was on the way home I made my big mistake. Jenna and me had never been close, even though we were the same age and had grown up in the same place since we were babies. Now, as we walked back, she linked her arm in mine.

'I'm glad yer not dead, Taney,' she said. 'I was so frighted I thought I'd throw up me breakfast. Finn's right: I'm an eejit of eejits, thinking you was dead, an' you just fast asleep.'

'I don't think I was asleep, Jenna,' I said, barely aware of what I was saying. My mind was racing, turning over what I'd felt and seen, trying to make sense of it.

'What d'ya mean? 'Course you was asleep.'

'My body was asleep, but some other part o' me was in the river, floatin',' I whispered, eager to tell someone, anxious not to let the boys hear. 'And it was beautiful.'

'Tell us,' Jenna whispered back. She put her head close to mine.

So I told her. I told her about the river's song, about the broken barrels on the riverbed, about hearing her screaming my name, about watching Finn and Jimmy trying to wake me and who said what. About floating up high in the sky and looking down on us all and thinking about going back to the river and floating out to sea.

'Lord God Almighty!' Jenna exclaimed, squeezing my arm tight.

'Shh!' I whispered urgently, suddenly realising how strange it all sounded. 'It has to be a secret; you mustn't tell anyone, Jenna. Promise.'

Jenna promised, and as soon as she got home she straight told her mam.

And Missus Mooney told Mary Kate.

And Mary Kate came in the door, white as a sheet, and told Da she couldn't have me in the house any more. There was a row the like of which I'd never heard, then Mary Kate grabbed Jon Jon and left, slamming the door behind her.

Silence stretched between Da and me. When I finally dared to look up, I could have died for shame. Da's eyes were all pain, like I'd hurt him real bad. His mouth was moving but he couldn't seem to trust himself to speak out loud.

'Please, Da,' I said. 'Please. I didn't mean to do it. It just happened. I'll never do it again, I promise, never.'

He groaned and closed his eyes. 'Jenna Mooney said you said it was beautiful, what you done. She said you said you wanted to float clean away. Did you say that? Did you think that, Taney?'

I began to shiver. 'I . . . It *was* beautiful, Da, but I won't do it again.'

Suddenly he was on his feet and across the room. He grabbed my face between his hands. 'It's not beautiful, Taney. Don't you never think that. It's wrong, like Mary Kate says. It'll destroy you if you let it, just like it destroyed yer mam. You must fight it, d'you hear me?'

I made some choking noise that he took as a yes. He let me go and went to the door, grabbing his old greatcoat and hat on the way. I heard him go down the stairs and slam out into the alley. I cried till I was too tired to cry any more.

I tried to figure out what I'd done that was so wrong. Was it that I'd done something other folk don't do? Or was it that I'd told about it? What did Da mean when he said it destroyed my mother? Did he mean she used to float? Why did seeing my mother's gifts in me upset my da so? And it had been so beautiful, floating. How could that be bad?

Another great sob rattled through me. My head ached. It was evening, so I made up my bed in the window and pulled across the curtain that hid my sleeping place from the rest of the room where Mary Kate and Da and Jon Jon slept. When Mary Kate returned with Jon Jon I pretended to be asleep and she never came near me.

Da came home very late. I could tell by the noise he made stumbling up the stairs that he'd been drinking. I heard Mary Kate help him off with his coat and boots. I thought I heard me da crying.

'There, there,' I heard Mary Kate say. 'It's high time she was workin', she's plenty old enough. She's been let go her own way too much. Let me take her with me tomorrow and she'll be too busy for any more of her mother's strangeness to grow in her. It'll be all right, Milo, you'll see.'

My mother's strangeness.

In the dark, behind the curtain, I dropped my hand down and touched the small box stored beneath my window-seat bed. I kept little treasures in it, shells and stones I'd found by the river, and bits of ribbon. The key was always with me, hid inside my tie-on pocket. The box was very pretty, all covered with flowers my mother had painted on it when it was hers. I touched it now in the dark. I wished with all my heart to be good just like Da wanted me to be. I even wished to be good enough for Mary Kate. I wished to be rid of my second sight and I prayed I'd never ever float outta my body again.

Please, please, I begged the darkness.

But even as I lay there, wishing to be rid of my mother's gifts, I felt all torn and wretched. Surely it was wrong to want to be other than I was? As my hand touched the wooden locking box that had once been my mother's, wishing her gifts away felt like betrayal.

Mother, I thought. Help me. Tell me what to do.

Nothing happened. No answer came. The box got a little warm beneath my hand but that was probably just 'cause I was rubbing it. I could hear Da and Mary Kate and Jon Jon breathing on the other side of the curtain but I was alone. I thought of the river's song and wished, just for a moment, that I had floated away with it, to the sea.

5

Mary Kate woke me early next morning; Jon Jon was hanging off her hip, sucking his thumb. I looked around for Da but he was already gone to work in the Brunswick Street mill. My face was all puffy from crying and my eyes felt red and gritty. I said nothing, just dragged my clothes on and shoved my hair outta my face.

'Comb it and tie it back,' Mary Kate said. She handed me an apron. 'And cover your petticoat with this. You'll be comin' charrin' with me this mornin'.'

I shrugged to show I didn't care one way or t'other. But I did. Just like that I was become a working girl, with Mary Kate deciding where my every minute went.

We went cleaning at Missus Kenny's first. Her stock had to be reorganised every morning after the rummaging of the previous day's customers. Missus Kenny sat in the centre of the shop, dandling Jon Jon on her knee and issuing instructions.

'Gintlemen's garmints go over there,' she said to me, pointing. 'Ladies' things over there, stuff for childers an' babbies in that corner there.'

Despite all that'd happened I fell to this task with some excitement. I'd often dreamed of being let loose in Missus

Kenny's shop, but it had been strictly out of bounds before. Mary Kate wouldn't have it said that her kids went annoying the landlady, hanging about like the Mooneys, getting in the way. Now I was actually under instructions to look and touch the clothes just as I'd always wanted. Moths fluttered in my face and the musty smell kept making me sneeze. Most of the garments were fairly tattered and made of rough fabrics like worsted and workaday stuff in dark browns and grey, but there were treasures too. Gowns of coloured dimity and cotton, printed with flowers and pretty patterns, linen petticoats with lace trims, buckles, shawls and gloves that only needed a little mending to look almost good as new.

'Come on, come on, girly,' Missus Kenny said, chivvying me with a mock frown. 'We've not got all day for you to be perusalin'. Shop has to be ready for openin' soon as soon can be.'

Once all the clothes were back in their proper corners they were split up again into outer, middle and under garments. Shoes went on the floor in rows. The very best clothes were hung on hooks high on the wall, out of reach of mauling hands; they would be fetched down with a long stick if someone wanted a closer look. The worst rags, regardless of whether they were for man, woman or child, went in heaps at the back of the room.

There were shelves all along one wall. On these the hats and bonnets were displayed; there were some tatty parasols and even a gentleman's umbrella. Underneath the shelves were drawers full of purses, pocket books, buckles, ribbons, and bits and pieces o' lace.

Mary Kate busied herself dusting and cleaning the shelves while I helped Missus Kenny with the outside display.

We carried out baskets and humped out barrels, all full of clothes, then arranged them in front of the shop where folk could rummage around in them under Missus Kenny's watchful eye. Some of the finest garments were hung around the window and door to attract people inside; they were tied to little hooks so as thieving hands couldn't have them too easy.

When we were done reorganising the shop we moved into Missus Kenny's living quarters and cleaned up her parlour and bedchamber but not the kitchen. There was a girl name of Patsy came in every day to cook and launder for Missus Kenny and the Misses Davies, and the kitchen cleaning was her affair. When we finished charring for Missus Kenny we went upstairs to the Misses Davies' rooms.

The Misses Davies were all flustered to find me come cleaning with Mary Kate. Miss Ruth tried to give me a cup of tea and make me sit as I usually did, but Mary Kate was firm.

'Taney's a workin' girl now, Miss Evelyn, ma'am,' she said, and the Misses Davies hid their 'oohs' behind their handkerchiefs and tried to stay out of our way.

Cleaning the Misses Davies' rooms was fiddly, what with all the ornaments and fine things, and Horace thinking feather dusters were for jumping after. But I'd made up my mind to do this right so I watched Mary Kate from the corner o' my eye as she whisked about the room, and tried to imitate her. The Misses Davies smiled their encouragement all the while, but the minute Mary Kate went down to the yard to empty the chamber pots I flicked my feather duster a little too hard. A china shepherdess wobbled on its shelf, fell and smashed to smithereens on the floor. My eyes darted to the door but, as luck'd have it, Mary Kate was too far down the stairs to hear.

'Oh, oh.' Miss Ruth's face crumpled as she stared at the broken thing on the floor.

'Quick,' Miss Evelyn said to me, distracting Jon Jon with a box of buttons. 'Brush it under the cabinet before your step-mama comes back and sees.'

That wee shepherdess was Miss Ruth's favourite of all their pretty china things, but she got down on the floor beside me and tried to help sweep the shards out of sight.

'You'll cut yourself, Miss Ruth,' I said. 'Let me do it, 'twere my fault. Your lovely little shepherdess; it can't even be mended, it's smashed so bad.'

'It was an accident, Taney dear,' Miss Ruth said in her gentle way. 'But I do wish you could still come to tea with us, as you used to.' She sighed. 'I know Mary Kate thinks it's inappropriate now, but we'll miss your little visits.'

I paused. I knew I shouldn't even think of doing what I was thinking of doing, but surely there was no harm? Da had always made it plain he didn't want folks knowing about my second sight but he'd never made me promise not to use it, not like the floating. The Misses Davies were old friends; surely I could do just this one little thing with the gift I got offa my mother? It was all I had of her after all. That and my red hair.

'I'll try to come later, Miss Ruth,' I whispered. 'There's

something I can do that might make up for breaking your wee shepherdess.'

The two ladies looked at me curiously. I put a finger to my lips to hush them as I could hear Mary Kate coming back up the stairs.

Later that day, soon as I could, I made a great play of leaving the house to walk by the river but doubled back instead and sneaked up the front stairs. I took tea with the Misses Davies like I always used to, but this time, to the old ladies' delight, I had a go at reading their tea leaves.

6

'Floatin' Taney, Floatin' Taney,' the other kids in Smithfield shouted now when they saw me walking down the street.

'Floatin' Taney Tyrell. Rise up an' float, Taney,' they'd call from behind corners.

That was the way of it ever since the day at the river. The Mooneys had told the whole world what happened and for a while all the women and childer of Smithfield were whispering whenever I walked by. I was strange like my mother, the women told their kids. 'Stay away from that young wan,' they said. 'She's just lookin' fer attention, makin' up stories, tellin' ungodly lies about floatin' clean outta her skin. Stay away from her, d'ya hear?'

It didn't bother me much at first; I'd always gone my own way. Mary Kate was mortified; that didn't bother me neither. But the change in Da, that hurt me bad. Once, we'd been the best o' friends, back when I was little and it was just me and him. I'd had all his free time then, all his conversation, all his smiles. Now he couldn't look at me straight; what talk he had was all for Mary Kate, and only Jon Jon could make him smile.

The gossiping about my floating died down eventually. The women forgot, but not them kids. They had a new game to play and I was it.

'Fly away home, Floatin' Taney,' they'd whisper as they followed me down the road. 'Fly away home to Thundercut Alley.'

I'd say nothing. I didn't care what they called me, as long as Da didn't hear them. But if one of them shoved me or walked on my heels, then I'd turn around slow and give them the sign of the evil eye. It was Missus Kenny suggested it, when I told her what was going on.

'Iffen they think yer a witch then threaten to turn their eyes crooked and make their teeth go black,' she cackled. 'That'll see them off quick enough.'

So when kids came after me I'd make a circle with my finger and thumb, bring it up to one eye and peer through, keeping my face as serious as the grave. Then I'd lift my other hand and point and start to mumble stuff under my breath.

'Run!' they'd screech. 'She's a witch! She's a witch like her mam.' And they'd scarper down the nearest street.

Then came the day they didn't run.

I was walking through the alley and first thing I knew of them kids was a rotten tomato whizzing by my ear. They were hiding at the side gate to Missus Kenny's yard, a pack of boys and some girls. Jenna and Finn and Jimmy were there, hanging back behind the others. I recognised the girl at the front. She was big for her age, taller than the rest by a half a head, and a whole lot wider. I didn't know her name but I knew she was hard as nails. She stepped out in front of me, barring my way.

'Witch,' she hissed. 'Let's get the witch.'

The other kids didn't move. I started my usual mumbling and began to make the sign with my hand. One of the kids whimpered and I could feel them panicking.

In a moment they'll be gone, I thought, and I'll be safe home. But the bully girl swiped my outstretched hand away and grabbed my hair.

'She's a witch,' she snarled. 'Stone the witch, stone the red-headed witch.' She pulled my hair hard, forcing me over towards the wall. One push and I thudded against the bricks, near losing my balance altogether. When I looked back, all o' them kids had stuff in their hands. Not stones, thanks be, but spoiled fruit and vegetables they must have gathered from the cobbles on the square – bad apples and bruised tomatoes and cabbages that no one would buy.

'Tis just old rubbish, I told myself. Just hold yer nerve and you'll be all right. But my legs ignored me and began to wobble.

'Get the witch, stone the witch.' The big girl was shouting now, and the other kids joined in. They stepped closer as they chanted. They could see I wasn't going to cast a spell; they could see I wasn't going to fly away. An apple hit my shoulder.

'Witch!' Finn said.

I stared at him in shock.

'Witch!' squeaked Jimmy, and he hurled his smelly cabbage. I ducked and it exploded on the wall behind me.

'Witch!' shouted them kids, and they all fired their weapons at once. Some stuff hit me, some missed.

They'll go away now, I thought. They'll go away and leave me alone.

'Again!' yelled the bully girl, and them kids shrieked in delight. They ran behind the gate and were back in a blink, re-armed with rotten stuff. 'Stone the witch!' they screamed again.

Another hail of market rubbish.

Stay standing, I told myself sternly. Look them in the eyes.

But 'twas no use. Terror got the best o' me. My stomach turned to water and, before I could stop myself, I ducked to the ground and curled up like a hedgehog with my arms clutched tight over my head. I knew I shouldn't, that every last bit of their fear would be gone when they saw their witch down and shaking. They'd do their worst with me now. Through fingers and hair I could see their faces. They were whooping and jumping and running for more of their stinky stash. Only Jenna was standing back, her bad apple still in her hand, her face white, eyes darting from me to the big girl. Then the kids were walking purposefully at me again, more putrid weapons in hand. They didn't throw them this time; they came right up to me and Jenna's face was blotted out of view as they closed in. I turned my head towards the wall and drew my arms over my face. I was going to be hurt for sure – hands were going to maul and punch and pull. I tried not to cry out.

Float, I thought, fly away and you needn't feel a thing. Fly up into the sky and look the other way.

But I couldn't float at will, not then. The sky disappeared in a blur of kids.

Mother, help me, Mother, I said inside my head. I tried to picture her face though I couldn't remember it at all. Please, Mammy, I whispered. Please.

'Get off her, yez little tosspots!' a voice growled from up the alley. I heard something rattling and thunking and then the kids were falling to the ground about me. The big girl squealed and went down hard, clutching her leg. Jenna Mooney, the only one still standing, backed into the gateway, holding her mouldy apple so tight it squelched through her fingers and ran down her petticoat.

Through the middle of the kids moved a familiar figure, his face creased into a snarl and his dark eyes flashing. He was swinging two wooden contraptions left and right like clubs, catching one kid a bruising blow on an arm and clattering another on the leg.

'Get lost now, the lot of yez, before I beat yez black and blue!'

The kids howled and yelped and scrambled to their feet and, in a minute, they were all gone.

I uncurled myself from the wall and turned to thank my saviour. I knew who he was. I'd seen him around the market since I was a small. I'd seen him rolling along in his wooden bowl, propelling himself over the cobbles and dirt with his two wooden batons. I'd always been too shy to talk to him and now he was here, in front of me, asking if I was all right.

'I think so,' I said. 'My hair's full of tomato but I suppose I'll live.'

'Sure an' it's red on red,' laughed the boy. Dimples flickered in his handsome face. He shook back his long black hair and held out a hand to help me to my feet. His hand was big and calloused as Da's. Standing up I was taller than him, though he must have been at least seventeen years old.

I was shaking from the fright I'd got. I knew I looked like I'd rolled in a rubbish heap and I didn't smell much better than one, neither, but I felt like a princess in a story. Only there'd been no dragon, just some kids turned spiteful and mean. And, instead of a gallant knight on a fine horse, I'd been rescued by a boy who rode about in a wooden bucket.

A lad known to everyone hereabouts as Billy‑no‑legs, Billy‑the‑beggar, Billy‑the‑bowl.

7

'I 'll see you home, if that's where yer goin',' said Billy.

'I live just over there,' I said, pointing at our lodging house. 'But my step-mam will kill me if I go home like this.' I tugged tomato outta my hair and scraped some brown slime offa my petticoat. 'I'd better go to the stream and clean myself up.' I glanced back up the alley to check them kids were gone.

Billy's gaze followed mine. 'Would ya like company?' he said. 'I could do with some fresh air after a day workin' the market crowd.'

'Thank you.' I nodded gratefully. 'That lot is probably gone now but I'd be looking over my shoulder all the way for fear they'd come after me again.' I hesitated. 'My name's Taney Tyrell, by the way.' I watched to see iffen he'd heard o' me and my strangeness.

'Let's go, so, Taney Tyrell,' he said, and he turned his bowl, deftly pushing one of his batons into the cobbles and swivelling on it.

I rubbed away some snot and tears and went after him. Billy's bowl was a wooden thing, like one end of a whiskey keg chopped off from the rest, but with iron bits at the joins and rims to make it strong. The bowl sat on an axle with a wooden wheel on each side. Billy propelled it about with the batons he had used to belt the kids offa me. Each baton had four wee legs on it; he held the baton and pushed the legs against the ground. The bowl looked awkward and rickety and it made a fierce noise on cobbles but I'd seen him make it go very fast on dirt roads. Right then he pushed it along beside me at a leisurely pace, like it was no bother at all to travel in a bowl, like it was the most natural thing in the world.

'Afternoon, Billy,' a voice called out from above our heads as we turned onto Queen Street. A serving girl in one of the posh houses was closing the windows before evening set in.

'An' how are you, Daisy Butler?' Billy stopped a moment and smiled up at the girl. 'Well an' aren't you the sight for sore eyes, twinklin' above me there like the evenin' star come out early?'

'Oh, get away with you, you flatterer!' The girl blushed and giggled. 'Take more than your pretty words to turn my head, Billy-the-bowl.' She raised an eyebrow. 'An' who's that ragamuffin you've got with you? Will you look at the state o' her!' She burst into peals of laughter and withdrew into the room without waiting for an answer. My cheeks burned with embarrassment. I made to walk away but Billy winked and motioned me to stay. Sure enough, Daisy reappeared almost immediately.

'Wait there,' she called. 'I have something for you.'

Five minutes later Billy and me were walking on, eating a couple o' cherry buns she'd fetched from the kitchen. They were a few days old but good, very good if you've never had them new-baked. Further on along the street another woman greeted Billy and told him to call by next day.

'Themselves upstairs is havin' a fancy dinner tonight,' she hollered from the cellar window. 'There'll be plenty o' leftovers. Come by for breakfast, Billy.'

'I most certainly will, Missus Doran. Thank ye kindly, ma'am.' Billy attempted an extravagant bow and pretended to nearly topple from his bowl down the cellar steps.

'Oh, oh, oh!' exclaimed Missus Doran in some alarm, then roared laughing when she saw that he was messing. 'You're a right divil, you!'

Billy and me turned onto Oxmantown Green. A group of young fellas called hello and an old man nodded from his perch on a tree stump.

Everyone knows Billy-the-bowl, I thought. Look at them all going outta their way to greet him as a friend. I tossed my hair back and straightened up tall, proud to be walking beside him.

When we got to the stream Billy tipped his bowl forward, leaned on his hands and swung himself over the lip of the bowl onto the grass. He sighed and rubbed his legs, what little there was o' them.

'They get sore, in the bowl,' he said. He lay back, put his hands behind his head and closed his eyes.

I tried not to stare at where his legs should have been but I couldn't help it. Folk always said Billy had no legs at all but I could see that he had two small stumps wrapped round and round with the leftover lengths of his britches.

'I was born like this,' he said, as if he knew what I was thinking. His eyes were still closed but I felt my face turn scarlet.

'I . . . I know,' I said. I waded quickly into the stream and began to clean my hands and arms.

'What else do you know about me?' Billy asked.

'Well . . .' I hesitated, wondering now if what I'd heard was true or just little tattle folk'd made up.

'Go on,' he said. He opened his eyes and half-sat up, propping his chin with his hand.

'I've heard folk say as how you used to be minded by the holy nuns on Brunswick Street. And that you never had no mam nor da.'

'I had a mam, all right.' Billy laughed, but it was a laugh with bitterness inside it. 'The nuns told me she was a local servant girl. But soon as she caught sight o' me she dumped me on the good sisters' doorstep an' bolted.'

'And your da?'

'Who knows? Could have been anyone, maybe even a lord or an earl.' He grinned. 'Sir William Nolegs o' Smithfield, that's me.'

'Were the holy nuns kind to you?' I asked, hoping I wasn't being too nosy but dying to know all the same.

'Mostly,' he said. 'There was Sister Mary Peter; she always petted me an' called me special. Then there was Sister Brigid Christopher; she couldn't stand the sight o' me. She said me mam's havin' me, an' she not married, was a sin an' that's why I've no legs. Sister Mary Peter said that seen as the sin wasn't mine God would surely not punish me for it. Sister Brigid said that it wasn't for Sister Mary Peter to question what God did.'

'But Sister Mary Peter was right,' I said indignantly, pausing with my fingers tangled in my hair. 'I don't believe God would be that unfair.'

Billy shrugged. 'Don't matter one way or t'other. I still have no legs.'

'How long were you with the nuns?' I asked, examining all the bruises and scratches blooming on my arms. I'd given up on my petticoat; there was no wiping them green and brown stains out.

'I was eight when the sisters decided they couldn't keep me any more.' Billy fiddled with the long grass, pulled a few blades and began to chew them.

'And they just put you out on the street?' I stood up straight, appalled. He'd have surely been the sweetest little boy with huge eyes and black curls. Them nuns must have had hearts o' stone to abandon him.

'No. They didn't do that.' He made a face. 'They gave me to the House o' Industry.'

I gawped. The House of Industry was a place for the poorest and most wretched. There you had nothing, you were nobody. True, they fed you and gave you a bed, but you belonged to them. They made you wear House of Industry clothes and a button with House of Industry wrote on it so as everyone knew your shame.

'I was there 'bout two years,' Billy said. 'I kept tryin' to escape an' they kept bringin' me back. Then one night I got out an' dragged meself as far as the Phoenix Park. I hadn't really thought much on where I were goin' to; I just wanted to get away from that place.'

'The park?' I said, trying to imagine how hard it would be to drag myself all that way iffen I had no legs. I was sure I'd have got no further than a street or two before I'd have given up and let them find me and take me back. 'All on your own, and you only a little boy?'

'Tell truth, I had this daft idea that iffen I kept goin' maybe I'd find some kind family who'd take me in, an' I'd live happy for ever.' He snorted and glanced at me real quick. 'Stupid kid, I was. I didn't see a soul the whole time I was there. An' I was there near a week.'

'But what did you eat? Where did you sleep?' I asked, out of the stream now and sitting beside him on the grass. I could see his eyebrows lifting at all my questions but there was a glint in his eyes like he found my curiosity amusing. I didn't bother hiding it neither; I wanted to know everything about him. I wanted this afternoon to go on for as long as ever it could.

'I dossed down under bushes an' pulled leaves and stuff over me. I had some bread an' cheese I'd brung in me pockets, but it didn't last long. There were blackberries about, an' plenty a' water o' course, but I was starvin' most the time.'

'Weren't you scared?' I said, shivering as I thought how black-dark and lonely it would have been in the Phoenix at night.

'Terrified.' He laughed. 'I thought I was goin' to be ate by wolves or taken by a pooka, but after a few days all I could think about was how hungry an' cold I was. I rolled meself

41

into a ditch an' decided I'd let meself die rather than go back. Musta lain in that dank ditch for a day or more.'

In a wet ditch. For days. I wrapped my arms tight around myself. 'And then?' I said.

'I woke up middle a' night with somethin' snuffin' around me. Next thing I'm starin' into a fox's eyes an' it's starin' right back. I could swear it was thinkin', "I can take him, sure he's near dead already," so I let out a roar an' slung a lump o' dirt at it an' it scarpered.' Billy shrugged. 'I knew then that iffen I didn't want ta die I'd better get movin', so I started draggin' myself back to Stoneybatter before that fox returned with its friends.

'I made it to the village an' found meself an old shack ta hide in. I stayed there a while. At night I'd creep out to search for food.'

'Where?' I asked, not even trying to keep the admiration outta my voice. I'd never heard anything so brave.

'Rubbish heaps, the market square, back o' taverns and shops.'

I gulped. What he found there musta been very like the stuff I was trying to scrape offa myself right now. 'But you can't have got enough to eat that way?'

'I managed.' He shrugged. 'An' I was free. After a bit, people got to know me an' took to leavin' me out scraps. The House o' Industry wardens stopped lookin' for me so I began to take to the streets by day, beggin'.'

'And your bowl? I heard the smith at Jameson's Distillery made it for you.'

'He did.' Billy reached out and patted the side of the bowl.

'Best thing ever, it is. I took ta beggin' near the distillery when it opened first an' the smith would pass the time o' day with me. It started out as a joke, him sayin' as how it'd be easier for me ta get around iffen I'd me own wee carriage.

'I thought the smith was just blatherin',' Billy said. 'But he promised he would make me a bowl, an' he was good as his word. Took him a while to get the wheels right; he'd never made wheels this small. He got the cooper who makes the barrels at Jameson's to make the bowl itself. That first one broke up in no time so they reinforced it with iron bits. When I got too big for that one they made this, an' it's the best yet.'

'Is it easy to push about?'

'Me arms were already good and strong from swingin' meself about the place so I finds it easy enough. When you live on the street you carry your world with you. Before I got me bowl I couldn't keep nothin' at all. Couldn't keep a blanket an' I had to eat most what I got right away 'cause I needed me hands to get about. Now it all goes in me bowl with me. An' with me wheels I can travel further. It never does ta wear out yer welcome in one part o' town.'

'Did the House of Industry men ever try to catch you again?'

'They did, an' they still do, every now and then.' He patted his bowl fondly. 'But me grand chariot makes it easier to get away, an' folk hereabouts always do their best to hinder them chasin' me.'

I nodded. Everyone hated the House of Industry, and them that worked in it were despised by all.

We sat in silence for a while. I was thinking how courageous Billy was, even when he was only a little boy. I didn't think I could be so brave as to run away from all I knew, and me at least having two legs to run away on. I was remembering how he'd come to my rescue and saved me from them kids.

'So, what were them kids tauntin' you for?' Billy asked.

I blinked. He didn't know, then, about my floating. He didn't know how the kids called me a witch, nor what their mammies said about me. I thought about telling him the truth to see what he would say, to see if he'd think I was strange or if he'd still want to sit with me and talk. I decided not to chance it.

'It's 'cause my hair is red,' I said.

'The girls are just jealous and the boys are stupid,' he said. 'Yer hair's amazin'. It makes you different. Folks don't always like different but that's their problem, not yours.'

I felt myself flush pink with pleasure and let my hair fall across my face. 'You don't think it's bad to be different?' I asked, and then turned red completely and covered my mouth with both hands. But Billy just laughed. He laughed loud and hard, and I began to laugh with him. The two of us laughed so much it made my stomach ache and tears roll down my cheeks.

Dusk was coming in. It must have been about seven in the evening by then. I knew Mary Kate'd be annoyed at me for staying out past eating time and she'd be raging when she saw the state of me. But it'd be worth it. I'd had a good time at the stream and I knew them kids would leave me alone from here on in, I just knew it. I had my own defender now. Someone who thought it was all right to be different. Someone who might even become a friend.

8

For the next week I haunted the market square and walked all over Stoneybatter, hoping to catch a glimpse of Billy. I was sure, so sure, that we'd meet and he would talk and laugh with me, and everyone would see what good friends we were. I thought o' nothing but Billy. Then after a few days and no sign of him I began to think, maybe.

Maybe I was just a kid he'd taken pity on. Maybe when he saw me again he'd just say hello and pass on by. Maybe he wouldn't even remember my name. He didn't need another friend; I was the friendless one. Me.

Next time I left the lodging house I turned right, away from the square. No more looking for Billy, I told myself. Stop fooling yourself, Taney Tyrell. He was just being kind. He doesn't want a kid likes a you hanging around.

I ran up the alley, across the green, down the back lane towards the stream. I threw myself down in the grass where we'd spent that other day and remembered all the things he'd told me and the things I hadn't told him.

Maybe that's why I haven't seen him, I thought. He's found out about my floating and he thinks I'm too weird. Maybe—

'Tell me about the floatin',' a voice behind me said.

I hadn't heard Billy rolling across the grass. My heart took to pounding half outta my chest. I looked at him to see whether he was making fun o' me but I could see his smile was real.

'I didn't realise you was the girl all the fuss were about a few weeks back,' he said. 'You know they're callin' ya a witch one minute an' sayin' yer just a wee lyin' rossie the next?'

I nodded. I laughed and shrugged like I didn't care a toss what they said.

'So what's the truth, then? Did you float outta yer skin?' he asked.

I tried to read his face. What would he think of me iffen I told him the truth? Should I risk it?

'What's it like?' he insisted. 'Did it really happen?'

I stuttered and stumbled at first, trying to find the words to describe that day at the river. Even to my ears it sounded mad but Billy didn't scoff and say I was lying. He didn't say it was unnatural and wicked either.

'It could have been a dream,' I said. 'But I think my mother used to do it.'

'Wish I could do it.' Billy looked up at the sky. 'Wish I could see the world from up there in the clouds 'stead of down here in the dirt.' Then he looked at me sharply, like he'd only just heard what I'd said.

'Yer mam used ta do it? Someone told me yer mam had the second sight an' all. D'ya have that too?' he asked.

I nodded. That didn't seem to bother him none neither. In fact, he looked impressed.

'How come that's not known be all an' sundry, then?'

'Me da doesn't like it so I don't let on,' I said.

'But that's amazin', so 'tis,' Billy said, staring at me now like I was a wonder. 'How does it work? D'ya hear voices or what?'

I shook my head. Amazing. The word rang inside my brain. Billy thinks me having second sight is amazing.

'I just suddenly know stuff,' I answered. 'Whatever I've been doing or thinking gets pushed out o' the way and suddenly I'm seeing something happening inside my head. It's like ...' I struggled for the right words to explain the feeling that came with the visions. No one had ever asked me to describe it before. 'It's like something that comes into my head from outside. The pictures are inside my head but they don't belong to me.' I frowned. I'd never given it much thought before.

'Can you make it happen?'

'No.' I thought for a moment. 'Well, I read tea leaves for the Misses Davies sometimes, but most of the time I'm just making things up for them, stuff I know will probably happen anyways. Now and then I do see things but nothing special.'

'So you *can* make it happen?' Billy insisted.

'Yes, sometimes, I suppose.' I laced my fingers together and hugged my knees into my chest.

'D'you not like talkin' about it?' he asked.

'No. Yes. I dunno. I've never really talked to anyone about it.' I stared at my toes. 'I'm not supposed to.'

'I'll shut me gob if ya want.' Billy grinned. 'But I think it's great, so I do.'

I blushed.

'An' I told you all about meself t'other day. I suppose that makes us friends or something.' He put his head to one side and raised his eyebrows. 'What d'ya think?' he asked.

I smiled a smile so wide it fair threatened to split my face. I ducked my chin between my knees. Neither of us said nowt for a bit; we sat and watched the stream run between the fields.

'I'll bet iffen you really tried you could control that second sight o' yours, make it happen whenever you want it to,' Billy said. 'Think how useful it'd be. An' I bet you could float again an' all.'

'Maybe,' I said, but I was doubtful. That was a whole month ago. It felt like a dream now.

'Try,' Billy said. 'Try now. Go on, try.'

I laughed nervously. 'I couldn't. I can't.'

'Try.'

'Not with you watching me; I'd feel silly.'

'I'll leave you, then. Only promise me you'll try.'

'I promised Da I wouldn't.'

'Yer da won't know. Don't you want to float again? You made it sound like magic.' Billy stared wistfully up at the sky like before. I said nothing. I was struck as dumb as the buttercups that were all about me and I was glowing like one an' all. He turned them black eyes of his on me. 'You want to; I can see it in yer face, Taney Tyrell.' He picked up his pegs and turned his bowl away from the stream. 'Go on,' he said. 'Do it 'cause you can. Do it 'cause rest o' us can't.'

He bumped away over the grass and I watched him go, then turned again to the bubbling water.

Could I make it happen? I wondered.

49

I lay back on the grass, spread my arms wide and stared up at the clouds scudding across above me.

Float, I thought, float.

I closed my eyes.

Float.

I tried thinking of nothing. I tried imagining. I tried remembering. I opened my eyes again. The clouds were making me dizzy. Just for a moment it felt like the world had spun upside down and I was falling into the sky.

This is it, I thought. It's happening, I'm going to float again.

I could feel the excitement bubbling inside me. I wondered iffen it would be as wonderful as before. I thought how pleased Billy'd be when I told him.

Billy, I'd say. It was amazing! It was great!

Tell me, he'd say, tell me all about it.

I felt my body tense; my hands curled into fists.

Float, float, float, I chanted inside my head.

A bee buzzed across my nose and I jumped to my feet, flapping my hands about. I looked around to make sure no one had seen me.

Ninny, I scolded myself. You're a right ninny.

I started home across the green but I'd stood up too quick. Black spots flashed in front of my eyes and I stumbled. I knelt down on the grass a moment and leaned on my hands to wait for the spinning to stop.

9

A giggle gurgled inside my head. Jon Jon? Yes. Jon Jon laughing and running across our attic room in his white shift. Jon Jon kicking a wee pebble about. I saw him follow it under the table as it rolled over the floorboards. He caught up with it and kicked it again. It bounced against the wall and headed off around a chair.

Ah ha ha, went Jon Jon. Ah ha.

I smiled. Lovely Jon Jon. Then I saw the fireplace in the corner. The skillet pot was sitting on the flames, bubbling the potatoes for dinner. The pot had three legs and usually sat steady in the hearth, but in my mind's eye I could see one leg was hanging off its perch, a few feet above the floor. Jon Jon's little stone rolled past the wood pile and hit the bricks under the fireplace, under the skillet's dangling leg. Jon Jon on all fours now, eyes on the stone, hands reaching out.

'Jon Jon!' I was on my feet and running, running as fast as I could over the green, across Queen Street, ignoring the indignant yells of a pair of sedan chair men who had to swerve to stop themselves from tipping their customer into the dust.

'Watch where yer goin', you little brat,' the lead man shouted. 'We could ha' been a horse 'n' chaise, then where would you be?'

I didn't waste my breath answering him; I was already dashing along Thundercut Alley, barely avoiding folk and filth in my haste. I flung myself in the side door, my breath coming in big painful whoops. I had a stitch in my side; the stairs seemed to go on for ever. I hurtled through the door into our room and shoved a startled Mary Kate out of my way, ducking under the washing and belting my hip against a chair as I charged across the room. The chair hit the floor behind me with a crash.

There was Jon Jon, his wee hand closing on his new plaything; there was the skillet wavering above him, starting to tumble as Jon Jon's hair caught in the hanging leg. I grabbed his arm and jerked him back, rough and hard. I heard him squeal in surprise as we both fell backwards. I heard the skillet pot crash to the floor, the hiss of the boiling water on the wooden boards, Mary Kate's startled anger dissolve in a horrified gasp, my own yelp as my head came up sharp and hard against the table leg. Then all was quiet as we stared at the potatoes smashed on the floor with the steam rising offa them and the water seeping away. Jon Jon, who had landed mostly on top of me, blinked and hiccupped. Mary Kate and I watched as his mouth went from a tiny startled round mew to a huge, outraged O. He took a big determined breath in.

'Whaaaaaaaaaaaaa!' he bellowed.

Mary Kate reached down and scooped him up into her

arms. 'There, there,' she crooned. She frowned at me over his shoulder.

'I—I—' I began, ready to defend myself against her. 'I saw it happen. I saw—'

'I don't want to know what you saw,' Mary Kate said, kissing Jon Jon better. She looked at the scalding mess on the floor and shuddered.

'Are you all right?' she asked.

For a minute I thought she was talking to Jon Jon. I rubbed my head where it had walloped the table leg. There was a bump already starting. 'Yes, I'm all right,' I said.

She nodded. 'Sit over in your da's chair a minute then.'

I got gingerly to my feet and hobbled to the big chair that Da always sat in. Mary Kate plopped Jon Jon onto my lap. 'Hold him while I clean up,' she said.

She righted the fallen chair, wrapped a dishcloth around her hand and picked up the pot. She had just scooped the best of the spilled potatoes back in it when Da came in.

'Taney hurted me,' announced Jon Jon, and his lower lip began to wobble again. He held his arms up to Da who looked questioningly at Mary Kate. She began wiping the floor.

'It was my fault,' she said, without turning her head. 'I set the pot too close to the edge o' the fire and Jon Jon near pulled the whole lot down on his head.' She sat up straight but didn't turn around. 'Taney grabbed him out o' the way just in time and he got a fright, is all.'

Da looked at me sharply. He bounced and tossed Jon Jon above his head; Jon Jon's sniffs turned to giggles. Da's eyes moved from my tear-stained face to Mary Kate's stiff back.

'That's all?' he asked, his voice wary.

'That's all,' Mary Kate said firmly, and went on scrubbing the floor.

10

K eyser's Lane dropped away below me, narrow and steep, the dirt baked dry by summer heat. Running down it would be asking for trouble; rolling down it in a bowl would be crazy.

'Are y'on, then?' Billy said, rolling right up to the edge where the descent began.

'We'll fall, surely?' I moved my bare foot over the road's surface. In winter it would be a muddy mess but today it was hard and unforgiving. If either of us tumbled, that road'd skin us for sure.

'They don't call it Kiss-arse-lane for nothin'.' Billy laughed. 'Are ya too scared to do it, then?' He was shading his eyes from the evening sun so I couldn't quite see the expression in them. I heard the challenge in his voice though.

We'd been meeting every other evening at the stream for a couple of weeks now. Talking and laughing, sitting together in the grass. Now it was Billy asking the questions. Had I had another row with Mary Kate? Had I seen anything inside my head, in the tea leaves? Had I floated again? I soaked up all his interest like a flower sitting in the sun. Them evenings with Billy were the very best bits of my week, so that day when Billy suddenly said as how he was sick of the stream and its constant babbling, my heart had sunk down to my heels.

Was he tired of me too? I wondered. Was I boring him with my kid's prattle?

'Let's go somewhere else this evenin'. Let's do somethin' else, eh?' he'd said.

'Somewhere else? Where?' I'd stammered.

'Somewhere that isn't here,' he'd answered, chucking a stone into the stream. It hit the water with a smack. 'Unless, o' course, yer ashamed to be seen with me?'

'What?' I had blinked in surprise. 'Me? Ashamed to be seen with you? Don't be daft.'

He'd laughed then. 'Follow me to the ends o' the Earth, would ya?' I'd felt my face turn bright red.

'How about across the Bloody Bridge to t'other side o' the river?' he'd said. 'Will you follow me that far, Taney Tyrell?'

So, here we were, top o' Kiss-arse-lane, the steepest street in all the city. It began at New Gate, just past Cut-Purse Row, and plunged straight down from there to Cook Street. The bockety old houses seemed to lean back uneasily, as if they were afraid that iffen they relaxed at all, they'd slide all the way to the river and be done with it.

And Billy was proposing we go down it fast as we could, me on my feet and him in his bowl.

'But once we start there'll be no stopping, Billy,' I protested.

'Exactly!' He had a glint in his eye now and I knew he was going to run it, whether I did or no. He was rocking his bowl forwards and back, balancing it with his batons.

It's a test, I thought. He'll be disappointed in me if I don't run it with him.

'I won't think any less of ya iffen you don't do it,' he said, like he knew just what I was thinking. But I didn't believe him. His eyes were looking down that hill like nothing else existed in the whole world. I didn't want to see them eyes cloud over.

'I'll do it,' I said.

'Good girl,' he said. 'I knew you would. Let's go, then.'

To my surprise he pulled his bowl away from the edge of the drop, backing up till he was at least two yards off.

'What are you doing?' I asked, though I knew only too well what.

'Gettin' a decent start,' he said. 'Come on.'

I followed him back.

'This should do it.' He planted the batons firmly on the ground and began to roll the bowl back and forth again. 'Ready?' he said, grinning at me. 'One, two, three, go!'

He shot forward in the bowl, digging into the ground as fast and hard as he could. I broke into a reluctant trot in his wake. He hit that hilltop and flew over it, tucking the batons under his oxters and grabbing the sides of his bowl just as the wheels left the ground.

'Billy!' I yelled and I ran after him.

Suddenly it felt like someone had taken the world and tipped it sideways, and me and Billy were going to drop clean off. I threw my arms out to either side to catch my balance and tried to pull myself up but there was no stopping now. My legs were racing helplessly under me, feet thumping down on the hard clay, my arms flailing about. The more I tried to slow down and pull back my head, the closer I came to smashing down straight onto my snot. The lane narrowed even more as it went down, window casements hanging outta the houses on either side, like old friends reaching over, whispering secrets. A black hound with a mean look in its eye sprang from under one and made a snap at my ankles. I yelped in fright and grazed my elbow offa a wall. A gang of kids stopped their game and stared. An old man dozing in a window jumped in his sleep as I passed.

'Let go!' yelled Billy. 'Fly, Taney Tyrell, fly!'

I gulped and looked up. Ahead of me Billy was hanging on to his bowl as it shot along the road, wheels spinning so fast I couldn't see them at all. I gave up trying to control my legs and concentrated on Billy instead. Somehow my legs caught up on the rest of me and I was running a little straighter, running rather than stumbling.

Let go, I thought. Fly.

My heart was going like a hammer and tongs, blood roaring in my ears.

The bottom of the hill. A drain and a wall.

'Billeeeee!' I screeched. He was leaning back, batons in his hands again, dragging them along the ground to brake the bowl to a stop. I threw my weight back and tried to dig in my heels but over I went, rolling, bump, bump on the hard road into the drain. I grabbed at the plants growing there, using handfuls to jerk myself back from the approaching brick wall.

'Ow!' Nettles. At least the dung in the drain was dry. I brushed it off and jammed my stung fingers into my mouth.

Billy righted his bowl. It had toppled to a stop at the ditch and landed him out on the road. Three women chatting in a doorway clucked their tongues at us and turned away.

'Didn't I mention the nettles, then?' Billy smirked and handed me some dock leaves. I snatched them from him with a glare. 'Wasn't it like flyin', though?' he said, pulling me out onto the road. 'Isn't that worth a sore bum an' a few old stings?'

'Is it?' I said crossly, rubbing the dock juice into my hands.

'Beats staring at a brook,' Billy said, his face still glowing with the thrill of the hill.

'Huh. Maybe.'

'Don't worry.' Billy laughed. 'I'm not goin' to be draggin' ya here every day. Kiss⁄arse⁄lane is for special occasions.'

'What d'you mean?'

'It's for me black days.'

'Black days?'

He glanced at me then ducked his head just enough so as his hair hid his face.

'Some mornin's I wake up absolutely sure, sure as sure, that I can feel me legs. I'm certain that when I open me eyes, there they'll be, two fine legs, with feet on the end, just waitin' to be stood up on. An' when I stand on them, I know they'll start to run. They'll run so fast, they'll run me clean away from here.'

I stared at him and bit my lip. Somehow I'd got it into my head that seen as he was born without legs he didn't really miss them. Looking at his face now, hearing the bitter yearning in his voice, I felt sick to my stomach that I could have thought such a stupid thing.

'An' then I open me eyes.' Billy's laugh was angry. 'An' there's nothin' there, nothin' but two pathetic stumps an' this wretched bowl.' He whacked his hand so hard against the wood I winced. 'I grit me teeth an' get on with it, but I always promise meself that before the day's over I'll have a trip down Kiss-arse-lane to blow me blackness away. Otherwise I'd go clean cracked. It's the closest I can get to runnin' an' I don't care if I break me neck doin' it. I don't care, d'ya understand?'

I nodded. My eyes had filled with tears, which made him scowl.

'It's the nettle stings; they're killing me,' I mumbled, holding up my dock-stained palms.

'Life's for livin', Taney Tyrell,' Billy said, softly now. 'Even for the likes o' you an' me.'

I looked at him curiously. 'What d'ya mean?' I asked.

'Don't the sameness o' every day get you down? It do me.' He looked back up the hill. 'Sometimes you just have ta break out and do somethin' to put a bit o' life into the day.'

I nodded. Going to meet Billy at the stream had become that something for me.

'So ...' Billy dragged his eyes away from Keyser's Lane, 'Wednesday evenin', will ya come adventurin' with me again?'

Where? What? The questions began to form on my lips but I bit them back. I knew what Billy wanted me to say, so I said it.

'Yes, I will.' I blinked them questions out of my eyes. Of

course I'd go with him. Anywhere. The ends of the Earth, just like he'd said.

Billy smiled his approval. 'Wednesday, then. Meet me at the usual time, at the end o' Grange Gormon Lane.'

11

Grange Gormon Lane ran up the side of the flour mill Da worked in. I dashed by it quick so as not to bump into him coming home from work. Him and Mary Kate knew I was meeting Billy most evenings but I had a feeling that whatever Billy had planned for us to do tonight wouldn't meet with their approval.

Billy was waiting at the corner, his eyes dancing with that same glint they'd had t'other day in Keyser's Lane. I felt a few butterflies dancing inside me.

'Come on,' he said and began to roll up the road. It was a country lane on the edge of Stoneybatter. The mill stood at one end and an old inn at t'other, and a load of small houses squatted down one side, with plots of vegetables out the back. Beyond was nowt but countryside. It was quiet in the lane. No carriages, just a couple of horse and carts rumbling by, and not many folk about neither. I tried to guess what class of adventuring we were going to do here.

'Are we going to The Half Moon, Billy?' I asked, falling in beside him.

'Where else?' he said.

But when we got to the door of the inn Billy passed it and

swung off into the yard behind. Though it was mid-July and the evenings were bright, the yard was overshadowed by trees. I could hear a low babble of voices and, in the gloaming, I made out a large circle of perhaps twenty people, mainly men, standing about.

What were they all looking at? I couldn't see.

The air was heavy with pipe tobacco and the sweet smell of late honeysuckle and near everyone had a tankard in hand. A couple of wee children what should have been in bed by now were playing with sticks over in the corner, outta the way.

'Six!' a voice inside the circle said. 'The main is set at six.'

Gaming! That's what they were at. My eyes were out on stalks now. I was going to see real gamblers the like of whom I'd heard Missus Kenny talk. I'd heard her say gaming was rife in the city and all sorts of folk, high and low, were caught in its snare. Men were losing the very shirts offa their back, so Missus Kenny said.

Jay, I thought, Da'll kill me iffen he finds out I was hanging around gamesters.

'Stay close to me,' Billy whispered as he rolled across the yard. I nodded, too excited to speak. Them butterflies inside me danced some more.

'Evenin' all,' he said, nodding his head to left and right as folk moved to let him through.

'Evenin, evenin,' came the replies. People smiled and nodded back but quickly returned their faces to the centre of the circle where five men were squatting in the dust, staring at two small dice.

'They're playin' Hazard,' Billy whispered to me as one of the men scooped up the dice and blew into his hands. 'The one with the dice is takin' his turn at bein' the caster an' this is his second roll. Iffen he rolls a total o' two, three or twelve now, he loses, but iffen he rolls another six he wins an' takes the wagers.' He nodded towards a small heap of coins that sat beside the caster's feet.

The caster rolled the dice.

'Two fives is ten,' said one of the men. 'The main is set at six, the secondary's set at ten.'

'Did he win or lose, or what?' I asked, crouching down beside Billy so as I could hear him through the chat and laughter of the crowd.

'Neither, so he has to throw the dice again,' Billy explained quietly. 'He'll keep throwin' till he gets another six or ten. Iffen he throws a six first, he wins, iffen he throws a ten, he loses.'

The caster gathered up the dice. As I watched him blow on them again I realised, with a start, it was my da's friend, Matt Davern.

Go home, quick, I thought. Creep away afore he sees you. Iffen Da finds out . . .

I'd have gone an' all iffen it hadn't been for Billy. I didn't want to let him down so I made myself stay still. How long's it been since Matt Davern seen me last? I chewed a fingernail and tried to think. Two years, maybe three? He'll not know me; I'll be grand.

All the same I moved to one side so as I was mostly hidden behind a large woman in a red shawl. There was no sign of

Matt's old spaniel, but a young terrier was dozing a few feet away under a tree.

The dice hit the ground.

'Eight. Roll again,' instructed the man appointed to call the dice.

I peeped out around the red shawl; Matt Davern was sweating and his hands were shaking as he picked the wee cubes up. He blew on them once, twice, three times. I could see him mumbling under his breath but couldn't hear what he was saying. A prayer perhaps?

If it was, it wasn't answered. The dice rolled across the ground and came to rest, one face showing a four, the other showing a six.

'Ten! Pay up, Matt,' one of the crouching men said, grinning hugely. There were as many gaps as teeth in his grin. Matt Davern scowled at him and kicked the heap of coins beside his feet roughly so they all scattered across the dirt. The grinner and the other three men snatched up two coins each.

'Ah, don't be like that, Matt,' protested the grinner, gathering the dice up as well. 'Sure, an' I'll give you a chance to win it back in a minute.'

'His turn to be caster now,' whispered Billy.

'I wager a penny,' the grinner announced, and placed some coins on the ground. 'Who's in?'

Matt grunted and shoved two ha'pennies into the pile and the other three players did likewise. The new caster tossed the dice about in his hands a few times then let them fall.

'What'll it be?' Billy whispered in my ear.

'I dunno,' I answered.

'Take a guess.'

I shrugged, feigning calm though my heart began beating like mad. 'Eight?' I whispered. 'But I'm only guessing,' I added quickly.

'Three and five are eight,' said the caller. 'The main is set at eight.'

Billy's eyes glinted at me in the gathering shadows. 'Go on, what'll he roll next?' he asked, his voice so low I could hardly hear him.

I closed my eyes. I saw the dice. One face showed a two, the other a six.

'Eight again,' I whispered. We watched the dice tumbling across the dirt.

'Eight again. The caster wins,' said the caller, and the grinning man whistled happily and pocketed the wagers. He passed the dice to the bald man on his left.

This time I didn't wait to be asked. 'This man will throw ... five and then a ... two,' I hissed in Billy's ear. I could hear the excitement in my voice.

We waited and watched. The new caster rolled the dice. Five, then two. He lost his bet. I'd guessed it right. Only I hadn't guessed, had I? 'Twas my sight had done it. I'd asked it a question and it had given me the answer.

'I'm done,' the bald man said, standing up and dusting off his knees. He pulled a battered periwig outta his waistband and waved it vaguely at a cloud of midges swarming his bald pate. He plonked the dirty old thing onto his scalp so the pigtail was all to one side. 'I'll be off home before I lose this week's rent an' all.'

'Anyone like to take Ben's place?' Matt Davern asked, looking at the outer circle of watchers. There was some shuffling and shaking of heads.

'I'll play, Matt,' an old man said. 'If you'll lend me the money.'

Everyone laughed.

'I'll play,' Billy said, rolling his bowl a little forward. I looked at him in surprise, and so did everyone else. The crowd went quiet; someone snickered.

'You have ta have money to play, Billy,' Matt said, shaking his head and turning away.

Billy held up one cupped hand. He shook it and we all heard the unmistakable sound of jangling coins.

Matt Davern turned his head but he didn't quite look Billy in the eye. 'We'll not be takin' a beggar's money, Billy,' he said.

'Not so hasty, Matt,' said the grinning man. 'Hazard's best with more than four players, you know that. Let him in.'

Matt looked doubtful but the four players began a mumbled discussion. This seemed to signal a break in proceedings and some of the crowd moved away to fetch another ale from The Half Moon or take a wander further up the lane to answer Nature's call.

Billy grabbed my wrist. 'A tweak o' yer hair means the caster will win his throws, a flick o' yer petticoat means he'll lose, all right?' His dimples were flickering in his cheeks and his black eyes sparkled.

'What if I get it wrong, Billy?' I whispered. It was exciting to use my gift this way, testing it against this game of chance and I couldn't hardly believe the answers came so easy. But having Billy's money wagered on my getting them right, that was a different matter. Them butterflies inside me were fluttering something awful now.

'Don't worry about it.' He smiled at me. 'Let's have some fun, Taney Tyrell.'

'All right, yer in.' Matt Davern's voice boomed across the yard. 'Ya probably earn more beggin' than I do haulin' whiskey barrels anyway.'

'Maybe I do, at that.' Billy grinned. 'Thank you kindly, gentlemen, for allowin' me to join yez this fine night an' partake in yer amusements.'

'Ohh, don't he talk fine,' one of the women cooed.

'Get on with ya, Billy-the-bowl,' Matt Davern mock-growled. 'Save yer Blarney fer the street an' keep yer chat to call yer bets. Someone fetch a lamp; it's gettin' too dark to read the dice.'

The players reformed their circle with Billy sitting where the man called Ben had been. A couple of lamps were lit and the watchers came back and settled about the game. I moved myself around so as Billy could see me clearly and I was just out of Matt Davern's view. Them midges were dancing around my head now and I longed to scratch behind my ears but I kept my hands firmly folded so as not to send Billy any signals I didn't mean.

The next caster took the dice. Seven, eleven, I saw in my mind's eye. Billy had explained that that combination of throws always wins. I twiddled a hank of my hair. Billy hesitated, then placed a bet anyway. I frowned. Had

I muddled up the signals? But, of course, Billy had to bet that first time; he'd have been getting funny looks from the others iffen he hadn't. Next play I signalled him not to bet and he didn't. Next two plays I flicked my petticoat and Billy pocketed some coins. Then it was his turn to be caster. In my mind's eye I saw him roll nine and nine, a straight win. I flicked my petticoat.

Raise the stakes, I thought. Bet two pennies! Bet three!

But Billy kept his head and set the bet at one, like before. By now he had a fine wee stash of pennies and I was that excited I clean forgot to keep my arms folded between signals. Suddenly Billy was losing. Not once but twice, he placed a bet when I signalled him not to. Third time I grabbed a heap of my hair and swished it frantically this way and that, but still Billy laid a wager. His pennies were all gone.

'That's me done, gents,' he said, a rueful smile on his face. 'Thank ye kindly for lettin' me join yez.' He nodded at the players and they nodded back.

'Any time, Billy,' said one. 'Yer welcome, lad,' said another. 'Now, who'd like to take Billy's place this fine evenin'?'

As we moved away the circle closed behind us. I couldn't believe it had happened so quick. And it was all my fault. I was clearing my throat, trying to find the words to tell Billy how sorry I was for muddling him up and making him lose when I realised someone had followed us out o' the yard.

'Yer Taney Tyrell, aren't ya?' It was Matt Davern. His face was in shadow but I recognised his voice and his stooped shoulders. 'Yer Miles-high Tyrell's young wan, right?'

I nodded. This night that had started so well was taking a

tumble for the worse. I'd caused Billy to lose his pennies, and now my da was going to find out I'd been hanging 'round a crowd o' gamesters.

'Ya won't tell him ye see'd me here tonight, will ya?' Matt Davern's voice was anxious. 'Only, yer da don't think much o' gamin', iffen ya know what I mean.' He smiled a mite queasily and turned his hat in his hands.

'I'm sure Taney'll say nothin' to her da, iffen you don't,' Billy suggested.

'What?' It took Matt a minute to realise what Billy meant. 'Oh, aye. I see. Ach, there's nowt wrong with just lookin', young wan, so long as you don't take to gamblin' yerself, like Billy here.' He touched the side of his nose and winked at me, turned on his heel and wobbled back into the yard, chortling to himself.

I could see Billy's eyes sparkling in the dusky light.

'Wasn't that just grand,' he said. 'Didn't you feel yer heart thumpin' every time them dice rolled?'

'But you lost it all, Billy,' I protested, vexed near to tears by the thought 'twas all my fault. 'Did I mix you up? I got so excited I forgot to mind my hands. You lost all your winnings and all you started with too. I'm fierce sorry, Billy.'

'I saw yer signals just fine. You were great, we make a fine team.' Billy laughed up at me. 'I had to leave me money behind me tonight or they'd not let me play again. But you heard them; I'm welcome back. Next time we'll wipe 'em clean.'

'You lost deliberate?' As soon as he said it it made sense – t'other players would have been right sore iffen the newcomer they'd let join their game had left with all their money in his pocket. 'And what d'you mean, next time?' I stopped in my tracks as it dawned on me what Billy might be suggesting.

'There's only one thing'd stop us,' Billy said. 'How many folk know o' yer second sight beside yer da an' Mary Kate?'

'Only Missus Kenny and the Misses Davies,' I said. 'And they'd never tell.'

'And Matt Davern?'

'Da won't have said nowt o' it to him.' I pulled a face. 'He's ashamed I have it.'

'Yer mam had a reputation fer readin' folks' futures in the leaves but that's women's stuff, so most men would think.'

I nodded.

'I think we're in the clear, so.' Billy rubbed his hands together. 'We can do as we please an' no one will suspect a thing. Ha! Like I said, Taney Tyrell, we make a good team.' He rolled on down the street, belting along at a quick pace, still high from the evening's sport. I had to run to catch him up again.

'This Hazard game is regular, behind The Half Moon every Wednesday. We'll play again next week, you and me. And 'tween times we'll see what other mischief we can get up to.' Billy's laughter rang out loud in the quiet evening.

I said nothing. I was happy Billy wanted me around but I'd spent the last few hours with my heart in my mouth, worrying about what was going to happen next and iffen I was calling things right.

'You enjoyed yerself, didn't ya?' Billy stopped suddenly and peered at me in the dusky light.

'I did and I didn't,' I replied carefully. 'I was afraid I'd make a mistake.'

'But you didn't.'

'But I might have.'

'But you didn't. An' iffen you had, so what? Isn't it worth takin' the chance just for the thrill o' it?' Billy's head was on one side, watching me.

'What if Da finds out?' I said. 'Or Mary Kate?'

'They won't.' He smiled. 'You heard Matt Davern. Folks respect yer da and yer step-mam, an' nobody likes to be thought bad of. Them's that's out gamblin' don't want it known. They can't go tellin' on you without admittin' they were there themselves. Anyway, yer only lookin' on, as far as anyone can tell. No one knows yer as much part o'the game as them smelly old men.'

I giggled then. The guilt I was feeling o'er what Da'd think was fading away the more Billy figured that he'd never find out. 'It was exciting,' I said. 'It was hard work trying to keep the grin offa my face.'

'Yer tellin' me!' Billy snorted. 'So, we'll go again, next week? We'll only go iffen yer all right with it, though?'

I nodded. 'Next week,' I said.

'It'll be our secret,' said Billy, and he winked.

I nodded again. Our secret. I felt the thrill of it, of having something to look forward to, like Christmas, or my birthday, or Hallowe'en.

But better.

12

The next Wednesday we were welcomed back to the Hazard game as if we'd been expected. The butterflies were there again too but I enjoyed myself all the same. Billy and me were fooling them all. We were beating them at their own game and no one knew it but we two.

And I was using my sight. I loved the feeling of control it gave me to ask my mind what the dice'd show next and have the numbers pop into my head with no effort at all.

'Tis like when the Misses Davies learned me to read, I thought. The more I practise, the easier it becomes.

Billy didn't clean the others out, like he said he would. He kept the winning and losing fairly even so as he left the game with a couple of extra pennies in his pocket, but not as many as he could have.

'That's thrupence for you an' thrupence for me,' he said, handing me some coins.

I stared at them in surprise. 'For me?'

''Course,' Billy said. 'We're a team; winnings split fifty-fifty.'

That night in bed, behind my curtain, I turned the ha'pennies and pennies over and over, staring at the different

73

kings – Georges one, two an' three – I had them all. On t'other side were harps or naked ladies. I'd never had money of my own before; what we earned from charring was family money for buying food and fuel and paying the rent. I placed them coins quietly inside my locking box and turned the key, tracing my finger over the flowers my mother had painted.

Things had changed a bit since I'd started working a month before. Mary Kate had decided I could char for Missus Kenny and the Misses Davies on my own while she watched Jon Jon. He was getting too big and boisterous to bring with us. I'd come back around midday and mind him while Mary Kate went off to clean at the big houses on the streets where the Quality lived. These new arrangements suited me just fine. Missus Kenny worked me hard but she kept up her usual banter, chattering about her cousin in Meath and her younger sister what lived in Bristol, the price of coffee, the scandalous goings-on of theatre folk, and the latest fashions as worn by the gentry in the Rotunda Pleasure Gardens. The time passed quick as quick. The Misses Davies, on the other hand, would only let me do half what I should have and made me sit and take tea with them after that. Mary Kate'd have gone mad iffen she'd known. My afternoons were spent playing with Jon Jon and then, most evenings, I'd be off to find Billy.

At the Wednesday games behind The Half Moon, Billy and me played that crowd and they never knew a thing. The little cache of coins in my mother's locking box began to build up and somewhere along the way I began to think of it as running-away money. Ever since I was small and Mary Kate had begun her snapping an' snarking at me over what I hadn't done that I should have, and what I had done that I shouldn't have, I'd planned to run away. I used promised myself that someday I'd pack my box and leave, never come back, go where no one knew me and no one called me names.

Now, here the coins were, gathering in my box, and I found that I didn't want to go. Everything was changed. I had Billy. Mary Kate's sharp tongue didn't matter much at all, and I could even bear Da's coolness a little better, once I had Billy. I'd run away someday but not now. When I was older I'd have a fine amount saved. I'd be able to go anywhere I chose.

One evening Billy brung me to a cock fight in the old brick field offa Moore Street. The brick field wasn't in use any more and a pit had been set up inside the storehouse. There must have been a hundred people there. I'd never heard cursing the like of what I heard; not even the traders in the market would say such things. And the smell. I wrinkled my nose up in disgust. No amount o' tobacco could mask the stink of human sweat and stale beer. Wagers were being laid down all around us, faces suddenly sharp in the lamplight, hands flashing, fingering coins. The crowd jostled and hustled. I didn't like the leering looks some of the men were giving me. I tried to stick close to Billy. Next thing I knew some drunk had come a cropper o'er Billy's bowl and was sprawled in the dirt in front of us.

'Who let this blasted cripple in?' demanded the man, angrily snatching up his hat and staggering to his feet. 'Shouldn't be allowed, the likes o' him.' He spat at Billy before lurching away. I turned to Billy, all indignant. I'd never heard anyone talk to him like that before. I expected Billy to be angry but he said nothing, just wiped the spit offa his arm.

'Buy a girl a beer, Billy Bowl?' a shrill voice called out through the din, and we turned to see a group of women, standing together under a lamp. The one who'd called to Billy had a big, black beauty spot drawn on her chin but when she pulled her crimson lips back in a mock smile her teeth were black an' all. She winked at us and swung her hips and her friends burst into peals of laughter. I'd never seen petticoats hoisted so high, nor necklines so low.

'Billy,' I said. 'Them women—'

'Never mind them, come look at the birds.'

Off in the corners the fighting birds were being held in cages and crates, their owners watching over them, keeping them covered with cloths so as they'd stay calm till it was their turn to fight. Billy led me through the crowd, taking me close to each of the birds.

'Can you sense anything?' he asked, not bothering to whisper since we could hardly hear our own ears for the din. 'Can you tell which of them will be the winners?'

I tried to concentrate on one cage, tried to picture the bird under the cloth. For one moment I thought I heard the frantic flutter of a tiny heart but it was gone as quick as it had come. It was swept away by a sudden wave of excitement and want and impatience so strong I felt my knees buckle under me.

'What's wrong?' Billy caught my hand.

I gulped in a huge breath. Voices. Dozens o' them. My head was jammed with them all of a sudden. I bit down hard on my lip, using the pain to pull myself back to the surface and shut the door to my mind tight again.

'What happened?' Billy asked. 'Yer white as chalk.'

'It's like the feelings of half the room came in.' I shook my head as if that would toss out the last echoes of the invasion. 'But I can't tell nowt about the bird. I'm sorry,' I said.

'Forget it.' Billy looked shocked. 'I didn't know that could happen, Taney. I'd never have asked ya if I'd known that.'

'I didn't know, neither.' I gave a shaky laugh though I was fit to cry with the fright. 'It's never happened before.'

'Come on, we'll go home.' He put his batons to the ground and turned his bowl towards the door.

'No, I'm all right now,' I said.

I wanted to go home; I really did. But I knew Billy wanted to stay. He had that familiar glint in his eye.

You just need to take a few deep breaths, is all, I told myself. Calm down, push it away. Do it for Billy. Out loud I said, 'Let's stay. We may as well.' I moved to the pit and he followed me.

The pit was a rough circle dug into the ground, with a bit of a wall to keep the birds in and the crowd out. I was fairly horrified by the idea of seeing a cock fight but excited too, despite myself. The games out back o' The Half Moon were nothing to this. Here everything was raw and rough; it felt like the whole room could explode any moment into a huge brawl. Having it all inside my head had been terrifying but now I felt like I understood it better. Most everyone in the room was wagering money they could ill afford, and near all of them would lose every penny; but from the second they laid their wagers till their chosen bird won or lost, there was hope, wild hope that they'd go home tonight with coins clinking heavy in their pockets, coins that'd buy a new coat or a cut o' meat or pay a debt or mend a roof. Sure wasn't I building dreams on my winnings an' all?

The crowd began to yell; two birds were being brought into the pit. Everyone crushed forwards to get a better view. If we hadn't been right at the front we'd not have seen a thing; as it was, Billy had to hoist himself forward onto the wall, half-outta his bowl. We watched the handlers uncover the cages and pull out their birds. They held them up for all to see and the crowd cheered for one and yelled abuse at t'other, depending on their fancy. Then each man gripped their bird by the belly and began to circle and thrust them at the other, allowing them to aim a peck or a claw, building up each bird's fury to ready them for the fight. I suddenly caught a picture in my mind of the red bird, lying in the dirt.

'The silver bird,' I said to Billy. 'Wager whatever you have on it, quick.'

Billy didn't have to be told twice. He dropped back into his bowl and rolled away to find someone to take his money before the fight began for real.

It was well on by the time he had shoved his way back to me. The silver bird had ripped a huge cut in the red's breast; the red had near tore off the silver's right wing.

'Jay, Billy,' I gasped, ducking my head behind him. 'It's horrible, so 'tis.'

Billy just laughed, never taking his eyes offa the battle in

78

the pit. Both birds were exhausted, bloody, broken things when the silver rooster finally got the red by the neck and finished him. All the while the crowd was heaving and screaming, all the violence of everyone in the room concentrated inside the puny bodies of them two roosters. One moment I couldn't look; next I couldn't turn away.

We did well that evening. There were six separate fights between a dozen birds and I called each one right. Billy placed every wager with a different man so our unlikely winning streak went unnoticed and we both pocketed sixpence at the end of it. My running-away money was growing nicely, hidden in the locking box under my bed.

But that night my dreams were full of pecking birds and blood and the constant babble of too many voices. Faces flashed in front of me, their mouths opening and closing, but I couldn't make out their words. When morning came I could barely peel my eyes apart with tiredness.

'You were late home last night,' Mary Kate remarked, with a sharp glance. 'Where were you?'

'With Billy, sitting at the stream behind the green,' I fibbed.

'You're spendin' a lot of time with Billy these days.'

I shrugged.

Mary Kate frowned. 'He's a nice lad, Billy. I like him. But . . .' She paused.

'But what?' I said, trying not to let anger leak into my voice. I couldn't afford to lose my temper now, not when I was trying to cover up lies.

'Well, he's ...' She paused again. 'He's not ... well, he's ... different. You know what I mean.'

He's a cripple, is that what you mean? I near said it out loud. Billy's a cripple and I'm full of my mother's witchery. And you're a cow, and I hate you. But I pinched my lips together and said nothing, just made my face blank and acted like I had no idea at all what she was trying to say.

'Jenna Mooney's called for you a few times,' she said finally. 'I think she wants to make up with you.'

'She can want all she likes,' I snapped. 'Anyway, I thought you didn't like me hanging around with them Mooneys?' Mary Kate just raised her eyebrows and said nothing more.

The summer ran on. At thirteen years old I was an old hand at the long days and the warm nights, the flies, the bites, the constant thirst and the dusty roads, hanging about the river, paddling and playing. I knew to expect that the adults would get lazy and lax, that they'd tell you to be home before dark, forgetting that at midsummer it was light all the way to half past ten. All the kids in the city would be out larking about for ever, waiting and waiting for their mam to holler them home. On the really hot days the grown-ups got good and cranky from working; you learnt to stay out of arm's reach, 'cause you never knew when Mary Kate's crotchety would turn into a wallop that would catch your ear or leg.

Yes, I thought I knew summer well. But street games seemed childish and silly now I had seen the games adults played behind the inns and up the boreens when twilight fell.

Every week Billy'd tell me I was amazin', I was special, there was no one like me. I'd come home proud as a peacock though sometimes this new world that Billy was bringing me into seemed so queer and dodgy it made me dizzy. Then I'd be glad of the familiar things: playing with Jon Jon, Missus Kenny's chatter, the Misses Davies and their tea leaves.

Just as summer was running out, just when I thought I was getting used to my new life, everything turned topsy again. Da went to work one morning and came back almost as soon as he'd gone. The Brunswick Street mill was boarded up and locked. The owner had been declared bankrupt.

'Me job is gone, Mary Kate.' Da slumped into his chair. 'What'll we do? How will we pay the rent?'

I thought of the money in my locking box. I opened my mouth to tell Da he could have it, he could have all of it, but the words stuck in my throat and came out as a cough. How would I explain where it came from? And could I really give them away, my lovely shiny coins?

Before I had time to make up my mind what to do, Mary Kate scooped Jon Jon up into her arms and crossed the room. 'You'll get another job soon enough, Milo Tyrell,' she said, in a voice that would brook no argument. She plonked Jon Jon into Da's lap. 'Till then, you'll mind the child and Taney an' me will take on more char work. I'm always being asked to do more hours in the houses on Queen Street.'

She stepped back and put her hands on her hips.

'We'll manage,' she said firmly. 'We always do.'

So it was settled. The next morning I would go to Missus

Kenny's and the Misses Davies' as usual, and then I'd join Mary Kate for her afternoon rounds. I would go to Queen Street with her and learn to clean for the Quality.

13

I hardly slept that night.

Was it going to be hard to find time to see Billy now I'd be working twice as much? I wondered. That thought fairly made me sit up in my bed.

What if Mary Kate tried to use it as an excuse to keep me and him apart?

She'd never do that?

She might!

And Da. He'd looked so wretched when he'd told us about his job being gone that he seemed to shrink in his chair. It near made me cry to think of it.

But I was proud that I'd be the one helping keep us outta the poor house. What would I see tomorrow? How big and fancy would the house be? I finally fell asleep imagining rooms like the Misses Davies', only bigger, with shelves heaving with porcelain shepherdesses, and paintings all over the walls.

That morning I hurried through my usual work and then went to meet Mary Kate at t'other end of Thundercut, on Queen Street. As I crossed the road I could see her, busy cleaning the steps and the path in front of Number Eleven. There was a phaeton pulled by two horses standing outside the door. Mary Kate said it was for to take the ladies of the house on their afternoon calls.

She led me down the steps to the basement. 'We'll stay out o' their way till they leave, then do the bedrooms and the main rooms while they're gone.'

I nodded, barely listening, staring about me. We passed the open cellar door; it was full of rows of dusty wine bottles and coal. We moved through the scullery where a girl was cleaning a large fish in a stone sink, her hands covered in scales and gut.

A water pump right inside the house!

The girl barely raised her eyes as we squeezed by her. A blast of heat hit me as we stood in the kitchen door. A fire was blazing in the range, above it the carcass of a small pig was slowly turning on a smokejack. I could smell bread baking mixed with the sizzling pork. A crane with two large kettles had been pushed to one side. The room was heavy with steam and smoke. A tall wiry woman was standing in the centre of the room, pounding dough on the large table, flour rising in puffs around her. She looked up as we came in.

'Mornin', Mary Kate,' she said. 'Who have we here?' She wiped her hands on a cloth and came around the table to us.

'This is my step-daughter, Taney, ma'am,' Mary Kate said, pushing me forward slightly.

'Taney!' The woman raised her eyebrows. 'What sort of a name is that? Nonsense! I'll call you Janey.'

'Taney is the name my mother gave me, miss,' I mumbled.

'I see.' She sniffed. 'Ann Mangan's the name my mother gave me but I'll be Missus Mangan, ma'am, to you.'

84

Mary Kate jabbed a finger in my back.

'Yes, Missus Mangan, ma'am,' I said, though I could see no wedding ring on her finger. Housekeepers and cooks, it seemed, were all called missus whether they were or no, and Missus Mangan was both in this house.

''Tis your first time in a gentleman's house?' she asked.

'Yes, Missus Mangan, ma'am.'

She sniffed again. 'We're a small staff here. We go about our work above stairs quietly. We stay out o' the family's way as much as possible, an' you'll do the same. Always use the basement door; the front door is for them upstairs only. No starin' about, no chattin' and laughin'. If you do cross paths with a member of the family you curtsy an' say nothin'. Is that understood?'

'Yes, Missus Mangan, ma'am.'

'There's many valuable things in every room so you leave the doors open while you work.'

'Yes, Missus Mangan, ma'am.'

'Get on,' she said, and turned back into the kitchen. Mary Kate went into the pantry to collect the brooms and buckets. I peered in from the doorway. The shelves were loaded down with jars and bottles and there was a sugar cone stood beside a stack of honeycombs. Up above our heads, the rat shelf swayed, hanging from the ceiling where the vermin couldn't go. A half dozen dead pigeons and two rabbits lay on it, their heads dangling o'er the sides, their dead eyes staring down at me.

Mary Kate handed me the brooms and a bucket.

'That way,' she said, jerking her head in the direction of

the stairs. I stumbled up the steps trying not to brush the walls with my load.

At the return I stopped and looked back for Mary Kate but she was at the pump in the scullery, filling the other bucket. I began to mount the next flight o' stairs, drawn upwards by the light. In Missus Kenny's house the stairways were dark and poky, the walls were covered in old wooden panels and the house was filled with shadows all day long. Here the walls were pale colours and stretched high above my head. I could see a lovely arch at the top of the steps. Ornate patterns ran all around the edges of the ceiling and danced about a glass lantern hanging from the centre. Without thinking I walked forward. I was in the entrance hall – a whole room just for folk to walk through.

The light was streaming in through the glass fanlight above the grand front door. On the wall hung a painting of a bay, with boats and mountains. Underneath it was a small table made of dark wood. It had shells carved on it, just like the little tables in the Misses Davies' rooms, but there wasn't a brack on this one, not a mark nor a scratch. It was gleaming and smooth and stood there on curvy legs against the wall, all to hold a silver dish. A vase near as big as me stood beside the table. It was white with strange blue flowers painted on it and a small blue bird with a long thin beak.

The Misses Davies' things are pretty, I thought, but this! This is . . . I struggled to think of a word to perfectly describe what I was seeing. Elegant! That's it! Would I ever live anywhere so beautiful? I was still staring at it all when Mary Kate came up the stairs.

'What are you doin'?' she hissed. 'Get back here, quick.'

'Don't wander about like that, Taney,' she scolded as she led me up the next flight of stairs. 'And stop gawpin'.'

We reached the bedchambers two floors above. Mary Kate began to tell me what had to be done in these rooms but I was too awestruck to heed her now.

'Everything's elegant,' I whispered, trying out the word on my tongue. I'd never had much use for it before. With my nose in the air, I turned in a circle, staring at the candelabra hanging from the fancy ceiling. Mary Kate rolled her eyes.

'Gawk, if you must,' she said. 'Then strip that bed o' its linen.'

The bed was huge, four posted, with cream-gold curtains lined with red and a mattress so high and wide I had to use the little wooden steps at the side to stretch across and gather up the lacy pillows. Mary Kate drew back the curtains from the tall, tall windows and the light streamed in across the Turkish carpet patterned red and gold with glints of duck egg blue. It was much bigger and finer than the one in the Misses Davies' parlour.

'Here!' Mary Kate snatched the pillow out of my hand. 'Give it me.'

She let me stare my fill as she emptied the commode and wash basin into one bucket and washed and replaced the bowls in their stands. We made up the bed together, me savouring the smooth feel of the linen sheets and the soft wool blankets.

To one side of this room was the mistress's boudoir. Mary Kate gathered up the breakfast china and wiped down the little table. I'd never seen a table like it before. It was a very pretty box perched on spindly legs and the top had wings on it an' all.

'It's a Pembroke table,' Mary Kate said. 'Those side bits fold down and the box underneath is for holdin' the china and storin' Mistress Lacey's tea. Even Missus Mangan don't have a key to that box.' Mary Kate almost smiled as she said this. She didn't like the housekeeper either; I was glad.

We moved to the back bedroom. It was lovely too, all blue and white. There was paper on the walls with faint blue stripes going down and cornflowers printed this way and that. The bed was hung with blue and white curtains; the fireplace was tiled the same blue as the cornflowers. Mary Kate told me this room belonged to the daughter of the house.

'What age is she?' I asked.

'Fifteen.'

I felt my eyes widen. All of this space, this bed, these trinkets, these cushions and bows and ribbons, belonged to a girl just a bit older than me?

Mary Kate handed me a broom and I began to sweep the floor while she dusted and polished the dressing table. There was a full-length mirror standing in the corner. I moved the broom back and forth in front of it, snatching glimpses of myself as I passed. I'd only ever seen my face before in the old spotty cracked mirror in Missus Kenny's shop and in reflections in windows on wet days. This mirror was all clear and I could see a skinny girl in a faded green petticoat and a white charring apron looking back at me. When I'd first got that petticoat the sleeves were so long I used have to roll up the cuffs, and the waist of it swung around me when I ran. Now my wrists dangled several inches below the sleeves and everything was tight and short, with no more hem to let down and no more seams to let out. It looked old and patched and there were still ghosts of tomato stains from that day in the alley several months before. I looked gawky and awkward, my face pale and freckled underneath the white mob cap Mary Kate had made me stuff my hair into for working in the Quality's house.

I'm as plain as Missus Kenny says I am, I thought. Is this what Billy sees? And what else would he see? Hasn't he got eyes in his head? A plain as plain ragamuffin kid is all you are, Taney Tyrell, I told myself crossly.

I felt an ugly flush start in my cheeks. I turned away from the mirror but Mary Kate had come up behind me. I jumped, thinking she was going to scold. Instead she put her hands on my shoulders and turned me back to the looking glass.

'You need a new petticoat; that's grown too small and shabby,' she said, frowning. 'I don't know how we're goin' to get new ones but we'll have to do it soon or you'll burst clean out o' those.'

We stood for a moment considering our reflections in the beautiful mirror. Mary Kate, handsome despite her frown and her mob cap, and me, suddenly aware of what a pathetic figure I cut, here in this room full of fine things.

'Don't matter,' I snapped, dropping my head. 'I look a right sight anyway.'

Mary Kate snorted impatiently. 'With that lovely hair of yours? Don't be daft.' She pulled the cap away from my head with one hand and lifted my chin with t'other. 'Look at yourself, Taney Tyrell. I didn't know your mam but I seen her once or twice. You'll be a beauty like her yet.'

I uncreased my forehead and tried a smile. My skin *was* pale and freckled but with my hair it looked less sickly and more natural. And my eyes looked brighter without the white cap. Mary Kate fluffed my hair back into its natural curls and spread it out around my shoulders.

'Perhaps not *as* beautiful as your mam,' she said. 'But you'll come close enough when you grow into those cheekbones.'

The girl in the mirror smiled and the woman behind her smiled back.

Footsteps and voices – we heard them too late. We only had time to lose our smiles and turn our heads away from our reflection.

'Oh!' A girl, all shining blue eyes and bobbing brown curls, came through the open door and stopped abruptly at the sight of us, standing there in front of her mirror. Mary Kate turned scarlet, dropped her eyes and made a small curtsy. I did a quick imitation of her, keeping my head down.

'I'm so sorry, miss.' Mary Kate began to clumsily stuff my hair back into my cap. 'She ... I ... we ...'

'No, no.' The girl stepped forward. 'Leave it loose; let me see.'

Mary Kate hesitated, then slowly pulled the cap away from my head again. She stepped back as the girl came closer.

'What an exquisite colour your hair is.' I heard the girl's voice despite the loud thudding in my ears. 'What's your name?'

This seemed to be addressed to me. I looked uncertainly at Mary Kate who was standing with her hands behind her back staring at the carpet. 'Her name is Taney, miss,' she said. 'She's my step-daughter. We shouldn't have been lookin' in your mirror, miss. It won't happen again.'

The girl laughed. 'No matter, Tyrell,' she said. 'I look in it at least twenty times a day; I shan't blame Taney for stealing just one peek.' To my surprise, she winked at me and I couldn't help but return her smile.

'What are you doing, Clarissa? With whom are you speaking, darling?' More footsteps on the stairs; another voice. A woman swept into the room and I felt Mary Kate freeze beside me and stifle a groan. 'Good heavens, what's this?' the woman said, and she raised her already arched eyebrows. 'I thought we returned because you had forgotten your pocket book, and now I find you conversing with the charwoman?' She laughed. Her laughter had a brittle edge. I felt Mary Kate squirm.

'This is Taney, Mama,' the girl said. 'Look at her hair, isn't it magnificent?'

'It is indeed, darling. Quite lovely.' The woman paused. 'Lift your head, girl, so we may see your face.'

I raised my head. I looked from the girl to her mother quickly, then dropped my eyes again.

'Hmm.' Mistress Lacey put her head on one side as she considered me. 'The hair is lovely; the face plain.'

'Mama!' the girl protested.

'No sense in filling the child's head with nonsense, Clary,' the woman said. 'Though her eyes ... let me see your eyes again, girl.'

I was hot pink by now. I felt my fear and embarrassment become something like anger. I raised my eyes as ordered.

'Ah! There *is* some beauty there, I see it now. Unusual eyes, even if they *are* glowering at us.' The woman laughed again, genuinely amused it seemed. 'The periwig makers on Dame Street would pay you a pretty penny for those auburn locks, girl.'

'Mama!' Miss Clary said again. She blushed and glanced at me.

'Merely a suggestion, Clary.' She brushed her daughter's protests aside with a wave of her hand. 'Come now. Have you fetched your pocket book?'

Miss Clary collected the small embroidered bag from her dressing table. She smiled at me as she passed and they two were gone in a rustle of silk.

Mary Kate pressed my cap into my hands. Her face was taut and worried. She handed me the broom. 'Get on,' she said.

14

Now I was working all day every day, bar Sunday. I still saw Billy a few evenings a week, even though I was often so tired I could hardly think. Sometimes I'd make mistakes with my predictions but we always won far more than we lost. Billy bought himself an old greatcoat and a better blanket with some of his winnings. In my locking box my running-away money was growing. Billy always laughed at me when I talked about how I'd run away to London, for that was where I dreamed of going.

'London? Why London?' he asked, one day by the brook.

'Well, I don't speak any Irish at all, so no sense in running west o' the Pale. It'll have to be England,' I said. 'I figure London is just like Dublin, and I'm used to living in a city.'

'I'm thinkin' London is a mite bigger than dear ol' Dublin,' Billy snorted. 'An' it'll be full o' quare folks from all o'er the world, speakin' quare an' doin' quare things.'

'Exactly! So no one will care two straws iffen I'm different. London folks'll be *so* so-phist-icated they'll think second sight is only *dee*-light-ful and floating is . . . is . . .'

'The latest fashion?' Billy laughed. 'They'll be linin' up fer lessons an' payin' you be the hour! You'll be holdin' court in

93

fancy tea rooms an' salons an' gettin' your likeness painted by famous artists an' all.'

We hooted at the idea of it. 'But I do mean to go someday, Billy,' I said when we'd got over our laughing. 'Mary Kate says my gifts are from the devil, and I know there's plenty folk hereabout would think the same. In London I could start again. Iffen I wanted it, no one need ever know I'm different; I could be just like everyone else.'

'Is that what ya want, Taney? To be just like everyone else?' There was an edge in his voice that made me look at him closer but he'd let his long locks fall across his face and I couldn't see his eyes.

'Yes. No. I don't know.' I pulled a face. 'I'll go to London and make up my mind what I want when I get there.'

'What's holdin' you so? Off with ya ta London.'

'Not yet,' I said. A wee shiver of fear ran through me at the thought of leaving everything behind me and making that long journey over sea and land. 'But in a couple of years, then I will. I'll have enough money saved by then.'

'Ha! By then you'll have spent it all on a bonnet an' some silver buckles what'll turn out ta be tin,' Billy teased.

'I will not,' I said indignantly.

Mary Kate charred at three houses on Queen Street and one on Prussia Street. We went to the Laceys' twice a week. Though it wasn't the biggest of the houses we worked, I decided it was by far the smartest. But when we arrived this day all was strangely quiet down in the basement and there was a smell of burning coming from the kitchen.

'Where is everyone?' Mary Kate said as we looked about. 'Heaven's above, what are they thinkin' of, leavin' the fire untended?' She ran forwards and grabbed some tongs to push a stray coal back into the grate.

I plucked a blackening loaf from the griddle and put another that was almost cooked into the hastener. Mary Kate rearranged the cranes to prevent the kettles and pots boiling over. We went back out into the corridor and peered up the stairs. A voice wafted down to us: Mistress Lacey's voice, angry and sharp, though we couldn't make out what she was saying.

Mary Kate frowned. 'Something's happened. I wonder should we go up and find out what, or go home and stay out of it?' But she was mounting the stairs as she wondered so I said nothing.

'No one leaves this room until that necklace has been found!' Mistress Lacey's voice came from the dining room. 'And when I find it the thief will be punished. I have sent for the police.' There was a wail at that, the wailer of which I guessed to be Concepta, the scullery maid.

Mary Kate moved into the doorway which was a little ajar, pulling me behind her. Mistress Lacey was standing at the fireplace, her eyes furious. Miss Clary and her governess, Miss Hickson, were sitting on the sofa. Just inside the door the housekeeper, scullery maid, and Robert, the manservant, stood clustered at the edge of the Turkish rug. Missus Mangan was giving Concepta a shake to stop her tears.

'It don't mean nothin', ma'am, her cryin' out,' Missus Mangan was saying. 'Our 'Cepta never stole yer necklace,

95

ma'am. Sure an' the silly girl's not the full shillin', at all, at all. She's only afeard because you mentioned the pol√is, ma'am.'

'If she has done nothing she has nothing to be afraid of,' Mistress Lacey snapped. 'Who's that? Who's at the door?' She flapped her handkerchief at Missus Mangan to indicate she should move aside and let her see.

Mary Kate and me took one step in and bobbed our curtsies. 'It's our day here, ma'am,' Mary Kate said quietly.

'Excellent!' Mistress Lacey said. 'A valuable necklace has been stolen. As you and your daughter were not here when the wretched thing disappeared you are not implicated in its theft, which means you can assist in the search.'

Mary Kate's head shot up. 'Search, ma'am?' she stammered.

'Of the servants' rooms,' the woman said. 'They will all remain here with Clary and Miss Hickson. I will accompany you.' She stepped briskly across the room. 'We will start with Mrs Mangan's, as she is the senior employee. Give Tyrell your keys, Mrs Mangan.' She swept past us out the door.

The housekeeper stiffened and stared into the distance. She unhooked the huge bunch of house keys from her waistband and handed them to Mary Kate without even looking at her. Mistress Lacey was already out in the hallway. Mary Kate began to follow her but hesitated.

'Ma'am?' she said. 'Missus Mangan should come with us, ma'am.'

Mistress Lacey spun around on her satin slipper heels.

'Only, 'tis her room, ma'am,' Mary Kate continued. 'She

96

has a right to watch that Taney and me don't mishandle or pilfer any of her belongings. Ma'am.' Her voice shook but I could see by the set of her shoulders that she was determined to carry her point.

The mistress raised one eyebrow. 'Very well,' she said, and started down the stairs to the basement.

Missus Mangan's room was beside the pantry. She pointed to a key and Mary Kate unlocked the door. The housekeeper and her mistress stood aside as Mary Kate and me moved into the tiny room. It was neat as a pin, the bed made up, the small hearth clean of ashes, the old rug swept clean. To my surprise a small song bird was twittering in a cage above our heads. I looked about, wondering what the mistress intended for us to do. Mary Kate turned to her.

'Ma'am?' she said.

The woman had the grace to hesitate and turn a soft shade of pink. 'I suppose you must strip the bed,' she said. 'And check the mattress. And search any drawers and locking boxes.' Mary Kate began to tug at the blankets. 'And up the chimney,' Mistress Lacey added, warming to her task now. 'Also, check for cubbyholes, loose floorboards, and such.'

We set to and soon the room resembled a corner of Missus Kenny's shop after a busy day, for the mistress quickly made us abandon our attempts at putting all back as we'd found it. Missus Mangan's goldfinch was hopping around its cage scolding us shrilly through the bars. Mary Kate and me were red in the face – not from the work, though there was much pulling and lifting – but from the embarrassment of searching through another's private things.

It's wrong, I thought, what we're doing. 'Tis like we're making Missus Mangan stand about in her shift and we all staring at her.

And iffen we were red, Missus Mangan was fair turned purple by the time Mistress Lacey was satisfied that her necklace was not in the housekeeper's room.

Missus Mangan returned to the dining room and sent for Robert to watch while we searched his room in the outhouse. I don't suppose Mistress Lacey'd ever been out there before; she looked about her curiously, hankie to nose. Poor Robert picked nervously at one of the many pimples on his chin as we searched through his few possessions and the heap o' straw he slept on. We disturbed a nest of rats, was all.

Now 'Cepta was sent for and she followed us up to her attic room, sniffing loudly and swiping her nose with her sleeve. Her room was tiny and smelled bad; she hadn't emptied her chamber pot that morning. Mistress Lacey stayed well outside and we moved quickly through 'Cepta's meagre belongings.

'Fetch Miss Hickson now,' Mistress Lacey said to 'Cepta when we were done.

Mary Kate started in surprise. I, too, was shocked. Was the governess to be treated the same as the servants?

Two voices approached on the stairs. Miss Clary appeared, looking indignant, and Miss Hickson followed close behind, her face pale.

'There will be no discussion, Clarissa.' Her mother put her hand up to silence her daughter's protests before she could begin them. 'I kept Miss Hickson's room till last thinking we would have found the necklace by now and she would be spared the indignity. However, the necklace is not found and there is nothing to be done. I'm sure Miss Hickson understands.'

'Does she, now?' Mary Kate muttered furiously under her breath, low enough so as only I would hear.

I watched Miss Hickson's face as she stepped forward and unlocked the door to her room. Hurt and bewildered is what she is, I thought. She looks like a scared grey mouse. But she has no reason to be scared, surely?

The room was big, even though it was in the attic. The floorboards were decorated with coloured stencils, ovals and squares filled in with patterns of petals in pale blues and yellows. There was a dressing table, a wash stand, and an armchair placed in front of a small fireplace.

A letter lay half-written on a writing desk by the window. Something about it made me glance at Miss Hickson. I hadn't noticed how young she was before. Now I looked at her properly I'd guess she was no more than twenty. Her hair was the colour of honey but she kept it dressed simply and wore a lace cap that hid the most of it.

She's pretty, I thought. She hides her hair and dresses plain so as not to draw attention to herself.

Miss Hickson caught my glance; her hand moved to her heart. Her eyes darted to her bed, to the pillow on it, and I felt her alarm as Mary Kate stepped over to pull away the covers and begin the search.

It's not the necklace she's afeard of us finding, I thought suddenly. It's that letter on the desk. And in my mind's eye

I suddenly saw a bundle of letters, written in a man's hand, kept under the pillow. Letters tied with a ribbon and Miss Hickson's heart bound within.

Mary Kate tore back the coverlet and blanket and pulled away the sheet. I looked at Miss Clary and saw she was watching Mary Kate's movements with some alarm. As Mary Kate reached for the pillow Miss Clary's eyes darted to her mother who was drifting towards the desk where the unfinished letter lay.

There Mistress Lacey will read a name, I thought, a name she knows. And she will be angry. Miss Hickson will lose her place here. She will have nowhere to go. And all the time that necklace is in another room, one we've not looked in yet.

I was sure I was right and yet I knew I must say nothing. Like as not, they'd never believe me. And Mary Kate'd kill me. She was upset already; her lips were pulled in a straight line and there were angry red spots on her cheeks. Another glance at Miss Clary standing anxiously behind her mother told me that she knew Miss Hickson's secret. She caught me watching her now; she tried to hide her distress but I saw it just the same. Miss Hickson looked close to fainting, tears standing in her lovely eyes and her fingers wound around each other, biting the skin on her hands.

'It's not here,' I said suddenly, my voice echoing in the silence of the attic, sounding like a shout. 'The necklace — we'll not find it here.'

15

'Whatever do you mean?' Mistress Lacey said sharply, stepping away from the desk. Everyone turned to look at me. 'Whatever does she mean?' she repeated, looking at Mary Kate. 'You haven't even begun to search the room.'

Mary Kate glanced at me, her hand frozen on the pillow. I bit my lip. What had I done?

'Do you know where it is?' Mary Kate asked me, her voice a hoarse whisper, though she knew everyone was listening. I looked at her, taken aback by the question, unsure I'd heard her right. I could see she was boiling mad at this humiliation of our fellow servants. I could feel her fury at the part we were being made to play in it.

But she hates my second sight, I thought. She can't really mean me to—

'Can you find it? Can you make this stop?' she hissed.

I nodded.

She hesitated, then let go the pillow. 'Do it, then,' she said.

I closed my eyes a moment and concentrated. I couldn't see nor feel a thing but I had to get them all outta the governess' room, now I'd gone and opened my big mouth. 'It's not here,' I said again. 'It's . . . downstairs.'

Miss Clary moved in front of the desk, picked up the letter lying there, turned it in her hands, shuffled it together with some blank sheets, seemingly idling. 'Downstairs?' she asked brightly. Her eyes seemed to plead for my help.

'Downstairs,' I repeated, pulling the coverlet back up over the pillow.

Mistress Lacey looked from her daughter to me, and back again. 'What on Earth is your girl talking about?' she asked Mary Kate.

'Taney ...' Mary Kate began, 'she ... she sees things sometimes.' She looked at me helplessly. 'She has a gift, of sorts. She can read tea leaves and such.'

I blinked. Mary Kate knew about me reading for the Misses Davies?

'Do it,' Mary Kate said to me again.

Mistress Lacey's eyebrows rose. I saw her face work. She was curious. She was doubtful. She was ... amused.

'Are you suggesting we look in the teacups for my necklace, Mrs Tyrell?' she asked. Her voice was soft and low but her expression suggested that she wouldn't humour us for long.

I could see Mary Kate was already regretting letting her anger at Mistress Lacey's behaviour get the better of her good sense. Iffen she could have snatched back her words she would have. Too late. They were all staring at me now: Miss Hickson fluttering in front of the bed, Miss Clary still blocking the writing desk from view with her body. She looked as doubtful as her mother but happy to use any diversion to get us all out of her governess' room.

I took a deep breath and tried searching my mind again.

It's not in the attic? No. Definitely not.

Ah! There! I caught a twinkle, a glimmer, then it was gone.

It's somewhere in the house, but where? I put a hand to my forehead and feigned deep thought to try and gain some time.

Get them outta here first, I told myself again, then try and find the wretched thing. I moved to the door with my other hand stretched out in front of me and stepped into the corridor.

'Downstairs,' I murmured, as if I was in a trance.

It worked. They followed me, then congregated on the last two steps to watch as I decided which way to go next.

Concentrate, I thought. It has to be here somewhere.

Nothing.

'Oh, this is quite absurd,' Mistress Lacey exclaimed.

'Shh!' said Miss Clary. 'You're distracting her.'

Mary Kate's anxiety was coming at me in waves. I could hardly believe she'd asked me to use my gift; I think, right now, she couldn't believe it, neither. I made a show of moving my arms about, 'feeling' for a sign. My fingers brushed the door of the guest room. Something? Maybe.

'In here,' I said, with as much confidence as I could muster.

'It can't be in there.' The mistress looked shaken. 'The Honourable Master John Swandon is staying in that room. He would never do such a thing.'

'You were willing to believe Miss Hickson would,' Miss Clary observed. 'And what do we know of our dear guest, the Hon John, anyway?'

'His papa is an earl and they have a large estate in West Cork,' snapped her mother.

'And he is the fourth son and rumoured to have large gambling debts,' Miss Clary replied. 'I believe he only accepted your invitation because he heard we keep a good larder and a box at Smock Alley. What other reason could he have for condescending to stay with us, and Papa only a wine merchant?'

Mistress Lacey flushed, but she took the housekeeper's keys from Mary Kate, selected one and placed it in the lock. She said nothing to me, just pushed the door open. I took three steps into the room and stared about me.

The young man's things were everywhere. A portmanteau spilled out embroidered waistcoats and shirts and cravats onto the floor. A sea-green tabinet coat was flung over a chair and a yellow suit brocaded with silver lay across the bed, a dozen linen handkerchiefs tossed in a heap beside it. Assorted tins of snuff and scented wig powder were shedding their contents across the dresser.

Behind me in the doorway the women watched. I tried to reach for the necklace inside my mind's eye just as I'd reach for the numbers on the dice at the hazard games but I couldn't see anything. Why, now I needed so desperately for it to work, was my gift eluding me? All them nights with Billy, I'd been so sure it was growing stronger, that I had it under my control at last. Sweat began to trickle down my spine. Me and Mary Kate were about to lose this job, and probably all the other Queen Street work with it.

Find it! Find it, ninny! I screamed inside my head. My eyes

began to well up. What have you done, Taney Tyrell? Oh God, what have you done?

'May I be of assistance?' Miss Clary stepped into the room behind me. 'Shall I search under the pillows?' She walked past me and lifted the coverlet, turning to smile her encouragement. I could see she was grateful Miss Hickson was safe but unsure what I was up to, and why.

I shook my head. 'Don't touch nowt, miss,' I said, blinking back my tears, trying to keep my voice steady. 'Everything must be left just as though we've never been here.'

She nodded and moved to the windows. 'I will keep watch then, in case the stupid man returns. Will that help?'

I smiled shakily. 'Yes, miss. It will.'

I began to walk slowly around the room, comforted by her presence. I tried to concentrate on the necklace again.

Peacock, came a thought. Peacock.

That couldn't be right. What peacock?

I circled again. Sparkles glinted in the far corners of my mind, just out of reach. I tried to grab at them but all I could see was . . . a peacock. What did it mean? That the Hon John was a dandy? Well, we could all see that from the fancy clothes scattered around. I shook my head and tried again.

'Enough of this nonsense!' Mistress Lacey declared from the doorway. 'I must insist that everyone leave this room now.'

'A few more moments, Mama,' Miss Clary pleaded. 'What harm can it do?'

The necklace is in the peacock. The necklace is in the peacock. I didn't dare say it out loud, it sounded so daft, but I kept seeing the bird, all blue and green with its huge tail fanned out behind. I tried to push it outta my head and start again but it just came right back, only now there were words floating in front of it like a veil. I kept my back to the door so no one could see the panic on my face.

'It's here,' I said, forcing myself to speak the words firmly. I began another tour of the room.

Miss Clary was watching me, nodding and smiling, but I could see she thought it would all come to nothing.

Come on, Taney Tyrell, I told myself sternly and silently. Iffen you can tell which rooster is going to die next you can find a silly necklace. Iffen you're seeing a peacock then there must be a bloomin' peacock in the room an' all. Look again.

I closed my eyes.

Peacock. Veil of words. Miss Clary.

I snapped my eyes open and walked to the window. As I drew nearer Miss Clary my fingertips began to tingle.

'Would you mind moving, miss?' I asked shyly. She stepped to one side. Behind her on the window sill there was a cushion, left there as though someone had been using it to sit on. On top of it was a book, open and face downwards. I reached out and lifted it away. On the cushion, beautifully stitched in coloured silks, was a bird with a tail full of eyes.

'There,' I said, relief flooding through me. 'Inside the cushion.'

Miss Clary picked it up and shook it gently. Her steady smile turned to a wee frown. She looked at the seams; her fingers found a small gap. I watched in satisfaction as her blue eyes opened wide in astonishment, then admiration.

'Well, isn't Taney the clever one?' she said, as she drew a

golden chain from its hiding place. A diamond pendant came out last, and fell the length of the chain, swinging from her hand. She turned to her mother at the door, holding the jewel aloft so it shimmered in the light from the window.

We were quickly dismissed down to the kitchen with instructions to send up Missus Mangan and Rob to pack the Honourable's portmanteau and bring it to the hall. The Hon John found it there on his return and was loudly and coldly informed by Missus Mangan that the Laceys were no longer disposed to have him as their house guest. I was still trying to calm myself, aware how close to disaster I'd come, when two members of the new Dublin Metropolitan Police arrived. We all sat in the kitchen below, gazing up at the ceiling, listening to the footfalls and the murmur of voices. Missus Mangan had to hold 'Cepta by the wrist to stop her taking flight at the thought of policemen in the house.

I sat there trying not to shake. I was pleased with myself but it'd been a close run thing and I knew it. My mind was racing with all I'd seen and sensed, the secrets I'd brushed up against. The whole house had been laid bare before me, turned upside down and inside out.

Mary Kate and me are outsiders here, I thought. We should never have seen what we seen. And now that all's put back to rights we'll go home, like nothing's happened.

But I knew that wasn't how it would be. I could feel that I'd been drawn in under the household's skin somehow. My future had become interwoven with it in some way I couldn't clearly see.

107

We heard the front door open and close again, and footsteps on the basement stairs. Miss Hickson came into the kitchen.

'The police have been informed that a mistake has been made, that the necklace is recovered,' she said. 'They are gone, as is our house guest.'

Mary Kate was raging that the Hon John had been let away with it. 'Iffen it had been one o' the servants they'd have been into gaol, maybe even swingin' from a rope, just like that,' she said, snapping her fingers.

Miss Hickson shook her head. 'As the law stands I don't think he could have been prosecuted as he didn't actually remove the necklace from the house.'

'Them upstairs is always quick to point the finger at us down here.' Mary Kate was not to be mollified. She folded her arms across her chest and frowned. 'An' when it turns out to be one o' their own what done it, do they apologise for all the trouble they put everyone through, I ask you? No! The whole house upset, everyone's things ransacked, all for herself and her fancy jewels.'

Miss Hickson lowered her head and smiled faintly. She didn't agree nor disagree. She had a bundle in her hands and now she held it out to me.

'Mistress Lacey and Miss Clarissa wish to thank you for your assistance,' she said. 'They send you this gift and hope it will be useful to you.' She squeezed my hand as I took the thing from her, smiling her own thanks as she left the room.

Missus Mangan and 'Cepta pressed close as I opened the parcel. A taffety gown lay inside, white with tiny sprigs of lavender hand-embroidered along the neck and hem. It had hardly been worn; despite its fineness and light colour there wasn't a brack on it. I held it up to me, speechless with delight. It was perfect.

'Oh,' 'Cepta said, all cow-eyed. 'You'll look fierce pretty in it, so you will, Taney.'

''Tis not for her to wear they give it her, you daft girl,' Missus Mangan observed sourly. 'What use is a fine gown to the likes o' her, I ask you? Might as well give pearls to swine. They give it her to sell, and a pretty penny she'll get for it an' all.'

16

'It was beautiful, that gown,' I told Billy as I walked beside him to The Half Moon a few nights later. 'Taffety made by the Liberty weavers, Missus Kenny said. She let me try it on before we traded it in. It shimmered when I moved and when the Misses Davies saw me in it, Miss Ruth actually started to cry. I know it would have been daft to keep it but I wish, I wish, I *wish* I coulda.' I did a little dance as if I was wearing it still. Billy snorted. He was more interested in the Hon John.

'I wonder why he hid the necklace in the house after he stole it?' he said. 'Why didn't he keep it with him?'

'Miss Hickson said so long as the necklace stayed inside the house it wasn't stolen at all, as far as the law was concerned.'

'So he was probably out findin' a buyer fer it.' Billy nodded. 'Clever. He was puttin' his self at no risk until he was ready ta get rid of it.'

I ran in front of him as he rolled his bowl up the lane. 'You'll never guess how many things Missus Kenny gave us for that gown. This!' I flounced out the blue camblet petticoat I was wearing. 'It only needed a few small mends to set it to rights. And she gave me one with flowers all over, made o' poplin. That's for Sundays and special wear. *And* this neckerchief,' I touched my hand to the blue and red kerchief at my throat, 'Missus Kenny thinks there isn't so much red in it as makes it clash with my hair.'

I stopped dead in front of Billy, forcing him to a halt. I flounced my petticoat again and stamped my feet. 'And look, me first pair of shoes! They've probably had three owners afore me an' all, but a bit o' stitching from the cobbler has set them to rights. I've never had shoes before.' I gazed down at them, still amazed to see them there on my feet.

'Yer a sight fer sore eyes.' Billy teased, not looking at me at all. 'Some day ye'll have the dandies in Dame Street fallin' o'er themselves for ya. Now come on or we'll be late.' He put his batons to the ground again but I didn't move.

'Don't you think I look older, Billy?' I asked. I could hear the petulance in my voice. Everyone else had admired my new clothes.

He put his head on one side and regarded me. The familiar sardonic glint went outta his eyes for just a moment. 'You look very pretty, Taney, very grown-up,' he said, and he smiled at me, gentle-like. I let my hair fall across my face to hide my pleasure and stepped outta his path as he began to move on.

'And that's not all we got, Billy!' I fell in beside him again, enjoying the slapping sound of my shoes on the dirt road. 'There was a fine round hat and gloves for Da, and Jon Jon's first ever pair o' britches, an' all for that one pretty gown.'

'That was fierce generous o' Missus Kenny,' Billy said.

'She said it was worth every bit,' I insisted. 'Da was so pleased with his new gloves; his old ones were threadbare.

An' I think Mary Kate was so glad of getting all we needed without spending any money she forgot to be cross at me about showing my second sight to the Quality.'

'But you said she gave you the nod ta use it to find the necklace?'

'She did an' all. But that wouldn't stop Mary Kate being angry with me for having the gift to find it with in the first place.'

'Why'd she tell you to use it, then?'

'I think she was that embarrassed by Mistress Lacey making us search through everyone's things, for a minute she didn't care how it stopped, even iffen it was by my "mother's witchery"!' I laughed again, though I was puzzled by Mary Kate's silence ever since. She'd said nothing to Da neither. And nothing about my reading leaves for the Misses Davies. How long had she known that? I shrugged. Who knew how Mary Kate's mind worked? Not me. Why should I care so long as she wasn't harping on at me?

'But that's not the best of it, Billy!'

'What? Don't tell me Missus Kenny give you back the tatty gown an' all?' Billy gave a mock sigh.

'She did not. No, it's Miss Clary and her governess. We had to go back to Number Eleven the next day, seen as we'd done no cleaning, and they made a point of saying hello to me and asking me things.'

'What sort o' things?'

'How long I've had second sight. They're fierce interested in knowing what kind of things I see and iffen I can tell the future. They think it's a very fine thing indeed and say I am very clever ta be able to do it. They admired my new petticoat too. They made me take off my cap so as they could see it with my hair, and Miss Clary even let me look at myself in her mirror. And you'll never guess? I asked Miss Hickson to let me see her hair an' all! Miss Clary clapped her hands and insisted Miss Hickson do as I say, and we all stood looking in the mirror, one brown-haired, one red, and one yellow.'

Billy had stopped his bowl dead in the road. I turned. His face was clouded over; he was looking at me queer.

'What's wrong?' I asked. 'I thought you didn't want to be late to the game?'

'The servants in that house know, don't they?'

'What?'

'The servants at Number Eleven. They know how the necklace was found. They know that you have second sight. It'll be all over Stoneybatter in no time. That rightly puts paid to our schemes.' He glowered at me and his voice was sharp. 'They probably know at The Half Moon.'

'No, no, Billy, they won't,' I said, startled by his anger. 'Mistress Lacey made the servants swear they'd never tell about the necklace 'cause she says she'll not have common folk gossiping about her private business. She threatened to dismiss any one o' them that told.'

'An' you think that'll stop them?' His voice was still gruff.

'Well . . .' I faltered. 'They all live in, Billy. 'Cepta is from Wicklow, Missus Mangan has no family, an' Rob is real quiet. I don't think they go out an' about much at all.'

'They must have friends,' he said, but he raised his eyebrows hopefully, like it was a question.

I shook my head earnestly. 'Rob is silent as a ghost, 'Cepta is slow-witted as a slug, and Missus Mangan is a right bad-tempered old bat.'

He laughed then. 'Come on,' he said. 'We'll see what kind o' welcome we get at the game. They'll run us soon enough iffen they've heard anythin'. But you can't never tell those posh ladies that you come gamin' with me, d'ya hear?'

'No, never,' I promised, smiling back at him but my stomach was churning. Hadn't I come this close to telling them only that very day? Miss Clary was asking what I did with my time off and it had occurred to me how astonished she and Miss Hickson'd be iffen they knew I went playing Hazard and watching cock-fights and fist-fights of an evening. 'I'll never tell, Billy,' I said, as we turned in the yard of the inn.

We were welcomed to the game same as always. It seemed no one had said nothing; no one else knew about me having second sight than those did already. I put four more pennies in my locking box that night.

I fingered the coins and wondered iffen Billy was right and I'd spend them all on a bonnet, someday. Being with Billy was the best thing ever. And now Miss Clary and Miss Hickson were being ever so nice to me as well. With so much to look forward to every week why would I bother running away?

17

'Me a ghost, me a ghost!' Jon Jon sang, as I rubbed coal across his cheeks to blacken them, ready for Hallowe'en night. I tied an old piece of cloth around his neck for a cloak and he ran around the room flapping his arms. 'I'm flying, me a ghost,' he yodelled.

I began to arrange chairs around the hearth as Mary Kate lit a candle in the window. 'How many do we need?' I asked, herding our few chairs and stools towards the fire crackling in the corner.

'One for yer mother, one for mine, one for my father and one for my sister. Yer da an' me will sit on the edge o'the hearth and you an' Jon Jon can sit on the floor.'

Jon Jon stopped his galloping and came to watch me. 'Who's them for?' he asked, pointing to the empty chairs.

'That's for my mammy,' I said. 'And these are for your Granny and Granda Walsh and your Aunty Meg.'

'Them dead,' he said, screwing his face up into a puzzled frown.

'That's right,' Mary Kate said patiently, though she'd explained this five times already. 'It's Oíche Shamhna so the dead may come callin' on us. We need to show them that they're welcome home, so we light their way with a candle.' She pointed to the window. 'And we leave the door open for them an' keep a seat for them at our hearth.'

'But if the pooka comes?' Jon Jon asked, not sounding as brave as he had when he'd asked before.

'If any bad faeries come, haven't we got our own wee ghost to scare them away?' Mary Kate said, and she and me dived behind Jon Jon pretending to hide. This had been his favourite game today and we waited for him to strike a pose and growl at the open door. But it was dark now and his little lip began to quiver.

'Save us, Jon Jon,' me and Mary Kate cried. 'Tell that bad pooka to go away.'

'G-go away,' he quavered, flapping his hands in his ghost cloak.

'Hoo-hooooo dares tell me to go away!' boomed a voice from the stairs, and a large shadow blackened our doorway.

'Mama!' Jon Jon screeched, and threw himself into Mary Kate's arms.

'Boo!' Da put his head around the door and we all laughed. He'd been outside in the market place helping to build up the heap for the Samhain bonfire. His eyes were twinkling; I hadn't seen him in such fine humour in a long while. He took off his gloves, the ones I got him with the taffety gown, and rubbed his hands together. 'It's freezin' out there an' I'm famished. I'm goin' to eat up that grand pot o' colcannon yer mam has on the fire, all by meself.'

Jon Jon and me howled our protest and Mary Kate began to dollop out spoons of the lovely creamy mashed potato streaked green with kale, plopping generous scoops onto our plates. We had no sooner begun to eat when we heard scuffling and giggling on the stairs.

'Shhh!' we heard a voice hiss crossly. 'Yezzer not to talk. Yezzer to be as silent as the grave, so yez are.'

There was another small scuffle, then five assorted figures drifted into the room. The two biggest were covered completely in old sheets with holes torn for eyes and mouth; the other three had coal-streaked faces and an assortment of rags tied onto their clothes. The candlelight caught the whites of their eyes as they arranged themselves into a row. Jon Jon watched them from the safety of Mary Kate's lap, his arms wrapped tight around her neck. The tallest ghost cleared his throat.

'An' a wan, two, three,' he said, and they all began to chant:

'Give us apples, give us nuts,
Give us a share o' yer autumn fruits,
Give us milk an' bread an' butter,
Let us share yer Samhain supper!'

They bowed; we clapped. Jon Jon jumped off Mary Kate's knee and stepped bravely forward to have a closer look at the rhymers.

'Jenna,' he said, pointing at the middle-sized ghost. 'An' Tom an' Eamon.' He pointed to the two little ones.

'We're not supposed to talk to them, Jon Jon,' I whispered, darting Jenna a meaningful look.

Mary Kate stood and filled a plate with colcannon. She placed it on the table. They needed no further invitation, them

Mooneys; they fell on that plate of colcannon like it was the finest thing they'd ever seen.

'Finn an' Jimmy,' Jon Jon squealed, as the two older boys threw back their ghost sheets to wolf down their share of the plate.

Da handed each of them some nuts when they were done. Finn ate his quickly and held his hand out for more but Mary Kate slapped it away. 'Leave some for our other callers, Finn Mooney,' she said sharply, and the five of them took the hint and turned to the door. 'Thank you kindly, Missus Tyrell,' Jenna said softly. 'That's the best colcannon I ever tasted, so it is.'

As they left, two more small bands of ghosts drifted in. They sang their rhymes and were rewarded with nuts from the pile Da had gathered on the table. They didn't none of them get colcannon like the Mooneys. When I remarked on this to Mary Kate, she shrugged.

'Jenna an' her brothers are our neighbours, and I'm thinkin' they go hungry often as not,' she said. 'Givin' them a decent meal one day a year won't break us.'

It was time for us to go calling, now. Jon Jon pulled back as Mary Kate went to put on his little jacket.

'It's all right, lovey,' she said as she buttoned it up and pulled his ghost-cape out over it. 'We'll all put our jackets on inside out, an' them faeries won't know who we are.'

Da tamped down the fire so as it would keep smouldering while we were out and he smeared coal on his face and hands, making Jon Jon squeal.

'You an' me will scare any pookas that come to bear us

away,' Da said. 'Now, all quiet! We must creep down the stairs and frighten the Misses Davies!'

Missus Kenny was guarding the Misses Davies' doorway, handing out treats to the callers. She stood aside to let us through, averting her eyes and feigning not to see us.

'How'r ya, Missus Kenny?' Jon Jon asked loudly, surprised at being ignored by she who usually petted and coddled him.

'Shhh!' we all chorused.

While Horace's eyes glittered down at us from the dark up top o' the cabinet, we silently moved about the room, throwing huge shadows o'er the walls and pretending not to see the Misses Davies. They in turn fluttered their hankies about and spoke to each other and Missus Kenny of how a chill air had entered the room. We walked to the table which had a plate of pretty sweetmeats set out on it and helped ourselves to some sugared orange peel and toasted almonds.

'Lord God Almighty!' Missus Kenny shrieked. 'Look at that, Miss Evelyn, Miss Ruth! The food is liftin' clear offa the plate all by itsel'! There must be spirits abroad! Oh, oh, what'll we do?'

'Oh, oh!' the Misses Davies cried.

'Who will save us from these ghouls?' Missus Kenny hollered, clutching her chest and rocking forwards and backwards on her chair. 'They'll bear us away to t'other side, sure as sure, an' we with no good spirits to protect us.'

'I'll 'tect you,' Jon Jon shouted, his mouth stuffed full o' marzipan. He growled at the open doorway, waving his hands about, and we all laughed and gave up our dumb show.

Missus Kenny cut up the barmbrack and we each chose a

piece. For all the delicious raisins and nuts we nibbled it carefully at the edges, fearful of swallowing one o' the charms baked into the cake.

'Ha, ha!' Missus Kenny chortled, holding up a reed ring covered in crumbs. 'So I'm to marry again! That's what the year ahead holds for me, I don't half think!'

I spat out a cold lump wrapped in paper.

'Taney has the penny!' Miss Ruth clapped her hands. 'Taney will have good fortune and wealth.' I thought of the precious stash in my locking box and said nothing.

'I'll have no money in my pockets.' Da's mouth twisted into a wry smile as he held up a small rag he had pulled from his slice of cake. 'Well, the brack got that one right! It seems for now the women in my family will earn the coins an' I must play the housewife.'

'Sure, hasn't Taney already shown a gift for good fortune,' Missus Kenny remarked. 'That fine gown she earned herself has you all lookin' mighty handsome this Hallowe'en, I must say.'

'Aye.' Da smiled. ''Twas generous of her employers to gift her such a thing. We're dressed proper for winter, an' all thanks to the Quality's fancy fer Taney's red hair.'

Missus Kenny raised her eyebrows but said nothing. The Misses Davies exchanged looks. They all knew why I'd been given the taffety gown.

'Things are gettin' goin' down below,' Mary Kate said, looking out the window at the lanterns moving about in the market place. 'Stoke up the fire for the Misses Davies, Milo, an' we'll be on our way.'

With much thanking and warnings to mind out for the pooka, we went down the stairs and out into the lane. I was near as excited as Jon Jon. I hadn't seen Billy for a while but I'd see him tonight, for sure. On top o' that, I'd been charged by Miss Clary and Miss Hickson to store up every sight and story from the night to tell them next day when I came to Number Eleven, for the Quality didn't step out of a Hallowe'en night.

It was pitch dark and the lane was eerie and echoing with the noise from the square. We'd no sooner turned onto Smithfield when a gang of bad sprites in evil-looking masks bore down on us, howling like mad. Jon Jon took such fright Da swept him up onto his shoulders and promised he could spend the whole night up there, safe an' sound. We stood at the front of the lodging house and looked at the sight before us a moment.

A shiver suddenly shook my frame.

It was a chilly night but that shiver went right through me like someone had walked o'er my grave. I wished I could take Da's hand like I used to, but that would be silly.

'Tis nothing, I told myself, just the night that's in it.

Smithfield was full of people: folk dressed up in their best and others dressed as spirits and monsters and witches. There were screams and shouts as the disguised ones played tricks on their favourites and their foes. There was the din of hundreds of voices and above that came the calls of the criers selling apples and nuts, hot cider and cold, cockles and mussels, fried eel and such-like treats. Their scents filled the air, chasing away the sickly scent of mash from the distillery.

Mary Kate and me gasped at the size of the bonfire.

''Tis the biggest ever, Milo,' Mary Kate remarked to Da. 'It'll be some sight when they light it.'

The square was speckled with lights; I had our lantern clutched in my hand. I began to walk a little ahead of Da and Mary Kate, keeping my eyes peeled to see if Billy was about.

There it was again. Cold creeping up my spine, like an icy finger tracing my bones.

What is it? A vision coming? I shook myself. Don't be silly. It's just the winter biting. I scanned the crowd again. No sign of Billy.

A group of musicians played reels and jigs in one corner and some folks had cleared a space for dancing. I focused on the rhythm; I concentrated on watching the patterns the dancers were making with their feet. We stayed a while then moved on to the apple stall. The stall keeper had hung apples from strings for snap apple and iffen you could take a bite out of one with your hands behind your back, you got to keep it. Da won one easy but when I tried the apple shot away and hit me on the ear. Da bought some Lady's Fingers and a few Pippins. We stood to eat them and watched children apple-bobbing in barrels.

'Yer too auld for that, young miss,' the apple woman said, nodding towards the kids as they chased the apples about the water with their teeth. 'But perhaps ya'd like to use an apple to tell ya who ya'll marry?' She handed me a small knife. 'Ya have ta pare it all in one long piece,' she warned. 'Ya mustn't break the peel.'

I handed the lantern to Mary Kate. I started at the base of

the fruit and slowly worked my way to the stalk, careful not to let the peel get too narrow nor too thin. I held it up when I was done and it hung in a curl from my fingertips.

'Now throw it over yer left shoulder an' let's see what it tells us,' the apple woman said.

I did as I was bid.

'So what'd you say that is? I can't see it very well.' The woman put on a pretence of squinting down at the paring, though like as not, she didn't know her letters. 'Is it a C? 'Tis usually a C. Yer true love will be called Cormac, maybe, or Cornelius.' She cackled.

'No, ma'am, 'tis not a C,' I said politely, for the peel had snapped when it hit the ground and fallen one piece across t'other. ''Tis an X, I'd say.'

'X?' the woman exclaimed, leaning closer to look. ''Tis some quare fur-rin-er you'll be weddin' then, for sure. What decent Irishman would have a name began with an X?' She crossed herself with a shudder.

I thought of how I meant to run off to foreign lands some day. Maybe I would, an' all. I handed her back her knife, smiling to myself as I ate my apple.

We stopped next at a brazier where hazels and chestnuts were roasting and the smell was mighty fine. One girl was naming two hazels after herself and the lad she fancied, and watching to see iffen they moved closer together as they roasted, or iffen they shuffled apart. Her friends howled with laughter when the boy-hazel leapt clean outta the fire all together, near hitting the girl in the eye.

Beside them another hawker was simmering cider. Da

was dithering between which treat we should have with his remaining ha'penny so I put up my barmbrack prize to treat us all to both.

'I'll put my money back in my pocket so, if it's not needed,' Da said, his voice a little sour despite his smile. I bit my lip. I hadn't meant to 'mind him again of which o' us earned. I hadn't meant to knock the twinkle from his eye. I wished Billy would come.

We warmed ourselves 'tween the two fires as we ate them delicious things till the cry went up that it was time to light the bonfire. The din of the crowd rose and everyone moved to encircle the huge heap of firewood, turf and broken barrels that had been gathered in the centre of the square, tall as the tallest house, and just as wide. People began banging bodhráns and pot lids and anything they could get a noise from. We found a good spot and stamped our feet against the cobbles in time with the drums. My new shoes made a satisfying clack on the stones, though I was careful not to bang them too hard and undo the cobbler's stitches. The crowd pressed close. The thump-thump of feet and hands and drums rose to a crescendo. Some men stepped forward, torches aloft to light the Samhain bonfire. We each blew out our lanterns and, for one long moment, the whole world was black 'cept for the flaming sticks of the bonfire-lighters. Smithfield Square rustled and whispered and coughed itself down into silence. Only when all noise ceased did the bonfire-lighters move to the heap and plunge their torches deep inside it.

The darkness was thick about us. I heard Jon Jon whimper softly high up on Da's shoulders. I held my breath. The crowd waited. There was a whoosh; the kindling deep within the bonfire caught and cackled, tiny flames raced about and the heap exploded into a hundred small yellow dragons which grew and danced and leaped out at us. A thousand sparks shot into the air and the crowd roared, all of a one. Then the bodhráns were banging again, the fiddles struck up and everyone began to dance and run. Round the bonfire, round and round we all went, shouting, chanting, stamping around the fire, faces and masks flashing in the firelight, crazy shadows jumping and cavorting around us.

By the time we'd circled it thrice the fire had grown quite ferocious. The heat drove us back. We stopped our mad dance and stood around again, panting and laughing. Cows' horns and bones gathered from the knacker's yard sizzled and popped in the depths of the flames. On the top of the heap was a huge pile of horse skulls. Now they glared down with angry orange eyes. I stared at them, so dead yet so alive within the roaring fire.

A fierce wind blew up. Despite the heat of the fire, icy coldness gripped my spine again and this time I couldn't shake it off. I couldn't move at all. My breath caught in my chest. I rose outta my body, leaving it frozen like a statue below me. I felt everything around me fall away. For one brief moment I hung suspended above the square. The crowd became a hushed shadowy blur; there was nothing but me, the dead horses' heads, their burning eyes, and the howling wind.

Death, those flaming eyes said to me. Death, death, death.

My spirit crashed back into my body. I stumbled backwards.

Someone was tugging my petticoat.

'Are ya all right?' a voice said. Billy's voice.

I looked down at him and shook my head. 'Death.' I almost couldn't say the word. It stuck in my throat like it was trying to choke me. I pointed a shaking finger to the heads in the fire.

'Death's coming,' I whispered.

'Death?' he repeated, laughing.

'Don't mock me, Billy,' I begged, blinking back tears. 'I saw what I saw.'

His black eyes became serious. I could see the fire's reflection in them.

'Death?' he said again. 'Fer someone you know? Yer da? Jon Jon, Mary Kate? Me?'

I tried to calm myself enough to search my mind for answers. 'No, I don't think so,' I said. And yet I could feel the burning eyes of the horses pulsing through me even though I'd turned my back on them. I shivered.

'Yer sure it's not just the masks an' the darkness gettin' to ya?'

I nodded.

Billy took one o' my hands in his. 'This is the night the world o' the dead is closest to us,' he said slowly. 'But there's nothin' surer than death. O' course there'll be folks here'll not make it through this next twelve month. An' there'll be new wee souls comin' into the world fer their very first Samhain an' all. 'Tis the nature o' things. We can only hope it won't touch them we love sooner'n it should.'

He let go of my hand, patted his pocket and pointed into

his bowl which held an assortment of fruit and nuts. 'Not been a bad night's beggin'. Crowd have been generous. I've even got me some mulled cider.'

I knew he was trying to distract me. I could just about breathe normal now and my heart wasn't trying to jump outta my chest, but something was lingering. A feeling that death was going to brush close to me sometime soon.

'Something bad is going to happen, Billy,' I began. 'I don't know when or what but it must be something awful bad, 'cause I've never had a vision like that before. I think – I think I was flo—'

Suddenly Jon Jon was shrieking. Billy and me turned quick to see what was the matter.

18

A man was there, towering above Da, Jon Jon and all. The man wore a mask, all elaborate paint and feathers. He moved nimbly about on his stilts, swooping down on Jon Jon like a bird. The crowd around us cheered. Jon Jon waved his arms, all his fear disappearing as folk encouraged him to dance with the stilt man. Da jumped and jigged beneath Jon Jon and Jon Jon did his ghost-growl and clawed the air. The stilt man pretended to be afraid and the crowd laughed and cheered Jon Jon all the more, Billy and me with them. The man swooped again; Jon Jon and Da counter-attacked. The stilt man bowed his submission and Jon Jon punched the air, victorious.

'Me a ghost!' he yelled, and we all cheered once more.

The stilt man moved into the crowd. Behind him came a dwarf, cartwheeling and tumbling, and behind the dwarf, a woman, dressed all in shiny colours, with ribbons fluttering from her hair. All three of them spread out and moved in a circle, skilfully gathering a large crowd about them while at the same time clearing a space for themselves, each standing at a distance from the other and each claiming a part of the audience. Da and Jon Jon followed the stilt man; Mary Kate fell back to where me and Billy were, in front of the woman.

Why can't she'd leave us be? I thought, resentfully. As if what happened with the bonfire wasn't bad enough, now Mary Kate is spying on me, an' all.

The dwarf started a tune on a penny whistle. The woman reached into a bag hanging from her hip and took out two apples. She began to juggle them, one-handed.

'Sure I can do that!' Billy scoffed, grabbing some apples from his bowl and imitating her. The crowd laughed. I sneaked a look at the bonfire. The horse heads had collapsed into the embers. I turned back to watch the juggler.

With her free hand the woman took a third apple from her bag and tossed it into the air to join the other two. Someone tossed Billy another and he kept pace with the ribboned woman. She added a fourth apple, running them between both hands like they were on an invisible string. Billy tried that and came a cropper right away, all the apples tumbling down to the laughter of the crowd. The woman smiled, her hands never breaking their rhythm, them apples moving about her head. She began to make patterns with them, crossing some in front of her face, tossing one higher than the rest. I watched her, mesmerised by her skill and concentration, using it to calm meself.

'That's what I do when we go gaming, Billy.' I leaned down to him so as Mary Kate wouldn't hear. 'I concentrate and pluck out information from the players' heads. And then I juggle all them things I see till I know what move you should make to win.'

He nodded.

'But you got a fright just now?' Billy asked. 'Was it like what happened the night o' the cock fight? When all them voices rushed inta yer head at once?'

I hesitated. 'Sort of.' Truth is, I wasn't at all sure what had just happened. Had it been real or had I imagined it? Had I floated again? Iffen I had, it was nothing like that first time by the river. That'd been lovely; this time was like a really bad nightmare. My skin was still crawling from the shock of it.

'It took you by surprise is all. Next time you'll be able to stop it.'

'Maybe.' It had been so strong, though. And I'd been so sure I was in control of my gift at last. Was it growing?

Iffen it is, Taney Tyrell, I told myself, then you'll just have to work harder at mastering it. It's part of you. It isn't going to just go away.

I set my chin and the juggler winked at me like she knew what I was thinking. She tossed all the apples high, caught them one by one as they came down, and swept a bow. The crowd applauded.

'There's a bare knuckle fight at the old brick field tomorrow evenin',' Billy said suddenly. 'Will you meet me?'

The crowd's applause had stopped; his last four words hung in the air, loud and clear.

'Taney can't be meetin' you of an evenin' any more, Billy,' Mary Kate said, without turning her head from the juggler, who had lit some torches from the bonfire and was showing them to the crowd. ''Tis too dark and cold for her to be walkin' about the streets after supper.'

I looked at Billy in dismay. His face clouded but he shrugged.

'That's not fair,' I protested. 'You can't stop me seeing my friends.' I turned to Da who had just come back to us with Jon Jon slumped sleepy on his shoulders. 'Da?'

He shook his head. 'Mary Kate's right. Winter's here. Spring an' summer will come again soon enough. Meantimes you can see yer friend of a Sunday afternoon.' He turned his back and I knew there was no point arguing. Inside I was raging, though. Da'd never have said nothing iffen Mary Kate hadn't.

I turned to Billy. 'I knew something bad was going to happen,' I wailed. 'I told you!'

He half-smiled but I could see his dismay. ''Tis not the end o' the world, Taney,' he said. 'Not as bad as someone dyin', eh?'

I pulled a face. Truth told, I was fit to cry. 'What'll you do about the fight?' I asked.

'I'll go by meself an' chance me luck,' he whispered.

By himself? Without me?

'I'll still see you, but?' I asked, trying to keep the hurt outta my voice. 'Twasn't Billy's fault. He'd have to make the best of things; I couldn't expect him not to go just 'cause I couldn't.

'Of course. Am'n't I always about the place?'

'And we'll meet on Sundays?'

He nodded.

The crowd fell into a hush. Despite myself I turned to see what had caught them so intently. The woman had tossed the burning torches into the air and begun to juggle them, just like she'd done with the apples. Everyone oohed and aahed in amazement, waiting for her to burn her hands or drop one, but she never did. She moved backwards into the centre of the circle, spinning the torches as she went. The dwarf played his tin whistle, dancing about her and the stilt man joined them, circling the juggler, criss-crossing in front of her. Now the crowd were crying out and applauding and shouting their pleasure.

'That's what it feels like when I use my gift with you,' I whispered to Billy. 'It's like *I'm* taking charge of *it*, not letting *it* take charge of *me*. And I need to take control of it; I know that now. I'll miss it. I'll miss you, Billy.'

There was no answer. I turned to look at him but he was gone.

19

It's December, deep winter. I've been sneezin' and snotherin' in my window bed the past few days. Da an' Jon Jon have been looking after me. It's been nice, just me and them for most of the day while Mary Kate is out doing all the work.

I should feel guilty 'bout that but I don't. Serves her right. 'Cause of her I've only seen Billy twice since Hallowe'en, and second time I seen him he was in one of his black moods. He was a right crosspatch at first but he let me laugh him out of it, in the end.

'You're just missing winning all them pennies,' I joked him. 'Be sure you don't go losing your shirt. Missus Kenny says that's the way all gamsters go in the end.'

'I'm doin' just fine,' he said. There was a wee snip in his voice still, though he was grinning. 'A little skill goes a long way. I know what I'm at.'

Then the last two Sundays in November it went and lashed rain, so I couldn't go out, and Sunday just gone I was sickenin' with this cold.

I'm near to rights now and bored with lying abed. I've just had my first proper meal in a week and it's lying uneasy in my stomach. I know I should get up and fetch the bucket but

I curl up tight, holding my blanket against the cold of the night, and wait for the nausea to pass. I hear footsteps and look out the window. Someone is walking by on the square below. A girl, moving quickly over the cobblestones, humming to herself as she walks and pulling her shawl tight against the cold.

It's late, very late for a girl like her to be out walking the streets alone. By the look of her I'd say she's a live-out servant, going home after a long day working for the Quality. I follow her down the side of the square, towards the river end. Some drunks at the door of The Swan call to her but she ignores them and turns right at the Hay Market. The square is lit with lamps; here there are none. We're plunged into darkness. Her humming becomes louder and she walks faster, even though her brogues are slipping on the icy path. She crosses Queen Street at a diagonal and now she's moving along the Gravel Walk with only the moonlight to see her way. She stops humming and I can hear her teeth chattering. The houses are casting deep shadows and the girl's face flickers white below me as she walks.

She passes between the Bowling Green and the Gravel Slip; now she's on Barrack Street, walking along the big wall. The houses on the other side are petering out into wasteland.

She stops suddenly and I can hear her heart thudding. There's some bushes up ahead and one of them is rustling. She stares at it and it stops. She takes a deep breath and resumes walking, keeping as far away from that bush as she can. She starts to hum again.

'Uhhh! Uhhhhhhh!' It's coming from the bush.

The girl's hands fly to her mouth, stopping a terrified squeak. She looks down the walk, towards home. She looks back the way she's come. She is rooted to the ground as surely as the wall behind her.

'He-help me-e.'

'Who's there?' Her voice comes out in a whisper.

'I'm robbed and beaten and left for dead,' a frail voice answers. 'I'll not get up without your help, my dear.' A hand emerges from the bush, beseeching with its outstretched, shaking fingers.

The girl loosens her grip on her shawl and steps forward cautiously.

'Oh, your kindness, my dear,' the voice says. 'It shall not go unrewarded, I promise you.'

The girl loses her fear and leans down to grasp the outstretched hand. It closes on her wrist. Suddenly she's pitching forwards and another hand flies out from the bush. It seizes the girl's throat. She squawks and tries to pull away but the more she pulls the tighter the hand at her throat becomes. Her mouth is open in a scream, but she can only make small hacking noises, like the Misses Davies' cat, Horace, coughing up a furball. She's tearing at the hands clutching her neck; her feet are flailing about on the freezing ground, kicking helplessly at nothing at all. Her eyes are popping in her snow-white face; I can see the moon reflected in them, then her eyelids flutter closed, her mouth goes slack and she is still.

The hands leave her neck and move to her shoulders. They pull her towards the bush.

'Stop!' I find my voice at last. 'Leave her alone. Let her go.'

A hand grabs my arm; I hit it away.

'Taney!' a voice hisses in my ear. 'Wake up, for God's sake, before you rouse the whole house.'

20

I opened my eyes. Mary Kate was standing over my bed. Jon Jon was holding onto her leg, his thumb jammed in his mouth. They both stared into my face, their eyes as big as guineas, the light from Mary Kate's tallow candle sputtering over us all.

I sat up so quick my head reeled. For a minute I thought I'd throw up, I was that full of fear and horror. My hands caught at my throat. I was at home in my own bed.

'You've been callin' out in your sleep,' Mary Kate said. She felt my forehead. 'Are you sickenin' again? You're clammy as can be.'

I shook my head. 'I saw ... I saw ... I saw a girl being strangled on the wasteland by the barracks.'

Mary Kate frowned. 'Take a deep breath an' calm yerself, Taney. It was just a dream. Come on, there's some milk left in the jug. I'll warm it in the ashes and we'll all have a little. You'd like that, wouldn't you, Jon Jon?'

'What's 'trangled?' asked Jon Jon.

'Never you mind.' Mary Kate grabbed his hand and walked him to the hearth in the corner.

I sat on the edge of my bed and waited for the dizziness to

pass. It *was* a dream, I told myself, a bad dream. I stood up gingerly and padded out into the room. I was shivering, my teeth clattering together like them of the girl I'd imagined. Mary Kate put the milk jug down in the hearth and poked some life back into the embers.

'Isn't this nice?' she said. 'Milk at midnight!'

Jon Jon clapped his hands and giggled.

I looked at the straw mattress. 'Where's Da?' I asked.

'He went out for a drink with his pals from the mill; he's not home yet,' Mary Kate answered, her face tightening slightly.

I bit my lip. Since he'd lost his job, Da had taken to going out several evenings a week and coming home later and later. I shivered again. Mary Kate put her shawl around my shoulders and let her hands rest there for a moment.

'Who's first for warm milk?' she asked, letting go and bustling about the hearth.

'Me, me,' cried Jon Jon.

'Shhh!' Mary Kate said, laughing at him. 'Everyone else in the whole city is fast asleep.'

'Tell me a story, Mama,' Jon Jon said, sensing that tonight he might push his luck.

'Tell him about the time your aunt met a donkey on the road and thought it was her brother bewitched by the faeries,' I said. 'You used to tell it me when I was Jon Jon's age.'

'You remember?' Mary Kate looked surprised, but began to tell the yarn in a hushed voice, much to Jon Jon's delight. I leaned against the hearth and sipped the warm liquid from the tankard. The nightmare was fading, losing its vividness.

Jon Jon smothered his giggles and the shadows settled about us in that familiar room. When Mary Kate was done Jon Jon and me called for more. Mary Kate fetched a blanket and we all huddled together under it as she told the story of the stolen bride and one about the tinker's goat. We must have been sitting there an hour or more when we heard footsteps shuffling up the stairs. We all fell silent as the handle turned slowly and the door creaked open. Da blinked at us in surprise.

'What's goin' on?' he asked. 'What has yez up at this hour?'

'Taney had a maredream,' Jon Jon announced. 'An' she woked us all up!'

'Did she now?' Da smiled but his face was strained and grey. He pulled his hat off his head and laid it on the table. His hands were shaking.

'What's wrong, Milo?' Mary Kate stood up beside me. 'What's happened?'

'A girl has been attacked, near the Gravel Walk,' he said, raking his hands through his hair. 'The watchman found her an' came to The Swan for help. She'd been robbed an' strangled an' left for dead.'

Mary Kate's hand closed on mine. 'Left for dead?' she repeated. 'She's alive?'

'She is, but she can't describe her attacker or tell us aught about him.' Da shook his head and flopped onto a chair. 'What sort o' world do we live in, that a young girl can't walk home from work safely?'

'It's what you saw in your dream, Taney,' Mary Kate gasped. Her face turned pale and she let go my hand. I couldn't speak. It hadn't been a dream. It had been real. A girl was strangled and I'd been there, watching, witnessing. 'Twas so horrible, I couldn't hardly take it in.

'What's 'trangled?' asked Jon Jon, sleepy but trying to blink his eyes open.

'Time for bed, Master Jon Jon.' Mary Kate's voice was brusque as she picked him up. Jon Jon, knowing there'd be no more fun tonight, snuggled into her and stuck his thumb back in his mouth. 'Tell yer da what you saw,' she said to me as she moved to the big mattress. 'Make it quick an' quiet —' she glanced at Da '— then everyone must settle down for the night or there'll be no work done tomorrow.'

Da looked at me warily. 'You saw it?' he said.

I nodded. 'Just as you told it.'

'You dreamed it?' he asked. ''Twas a premonition?'

I shook my head slowly. It wasn't a dream, I knew that now. And it wasn't my second sight, 'cause that always came before the thing happened. This had been too real, too vivid. I had been there, at the Barracks' wall, watching it happen.

'You were floatin',' Da said.

I nodded slowly. I couldn't bring myself to look him in the eye. I knew what I'd see there.

'Were you floatin' on purpose?' he asked eventually. 'Or did it just happen?'

'I was asleep. I swear I couldn't help it,' I said. 'I didn't want to see what I saw. It was horrible.' My voice broke and I began to shake.

Da slumped in his chair. 'That used happen to yer mother sometimes, like she had no control over it.' He sighed and hid his face in his hands. I waited for the anger to come and hung my head.

Suddenly he leaned forwards, staring me right in the face. 'Did you see him, the strangler?' he asked urgently.

'No, no, I didn't,' I stammered. 'It was too dark; I only saw his hands.'

He closed his eyes in relief. 'Then we'll say nowt o' it to no one. There's nothin' to be gained by it.'

I nodded again.

'You'll tell no one what you saw, Taney, understand?' He grabbed my wrists and stood up. 'They'll only think yer makin' it up an' lookin' for attention.'

'I'll tell no one, Da,' I said, my voice breaking.

'Come here, lovey,' he said, and he pulled me close in a bear hug, like he used to when I was little.

I cried then and Da held me tight all the while.

'Da,' I said.

'What, lovey?'

'Tell me about my mother.'

He sighed. 'What do you want to know?'

'About her gifts. About her floating.'

He let me go and turned away.

'Her gifts killed her, Taney.' His voice had turned harsh and brittle. 'Her gifts killed her; that's all you need to know about yer mother.'

21

'I heard the girl is recovered but can't remember nothin',' Missus Mangan said as she humped the kettle off the crane.

'I heard 'twere the Pinkindindies done it,' 'Cepta declared, stopping her ladle of milk between pail and jug; our 'Cepta couldn't work and talk at the same time.

'Don't be daft,' Missus Mangan snorted. 'The Pinkindindies used hold up folk at sword point an' 'tis years since they were about. Anyways, the girl said as there was only one man, not a whole gang o' them.'

'Some say it was a furriner passin' through, an' he'll be left the country be now,' said 'Cepta. Missus Mangan was having none of this neither.

'The girl never said he spoke foreign; she said he spoke gentleman-like. No, he's still about. An' when he's spent all her wages what he stole offa her, he'll strike again, mark my words! Have you not got the milk in that jug yet?'

It was more than a week now since the attack on Barrack Street but it was still the talk o' Stoneybatter. I was listening to this kitchen prattle from a seat in the corner, where I'd been told to wait till I was needed. I twiddled my thumbs and wondered why I'd been sent for all of a sudden at eight o'clock in the evening.

Rob, the Laceys' manservant, had come to our lodging house a half an hour earlier, all outta breath and saying that he'd been sent from Number Eleven. The Laceys had guests that evening, he said, and 'Cepta had gone and got herself sick and was no use to anybody, so Missus Mangan was in need of an extra pair of hands, quick, quick.

Mary Kate had reached for her shawl but Rob insisted it was me that Missus Mangan had sent for, and me that must come with him. Quick, quick. Now I was here – apron on and hair stuffed inside my cap – and divil a bit was wrong with 'Cepta. I could see no reason why I had been summoned out into the night.

'Missus Mangan, ma'am?' I ventured, from my corner. 'Is there something I should be doing? Only Rob said you sent for me 'cause you were in need of extra help, ma'am.'

'*I* never sent for you at all!' Missus Mangan glared at me. ''Twas Mistress Lacey's fancy that you were needed upstairs.'

'What for?' I asked, startled.

'How would I know what goes on in that woman's head?' the housekeeper snapped. 'Orderin' tea an' cakes at this hour – who ever heard the likes?' She put the teapot of boiling water on a tray with a clatter and thrust the lot at me. I stood up and took it from her.

'The cups an' saucers is already up there. Themselves are in the back drawin' room.' She waved me to the door and turned away.

I set off up the stairs carefully, the tray with its heavy load of silver tinkling with every step. The drawing rooms were on the first floor. By the time I'd reached the door some milk had sloshed outta the jug and some of the fancy cakes had slipped offa their plate. I set the tray down on a nearby chair and did my best to set things back to rights. After straightening my cap, I knocked, hoisted the tray back up into my hands and shoved the door clumsily forwards.

There was the whole of the front drawing room to walk through to reach the smaller back room. As I rounded the corner my entrance was greeted by an explosion of giggles. Mistress Lacey was sitting at one of the little tables, Miss Clary at her side. Miss Hickson was hovering by the fire, her golden hair hidden, as always, inside a cap. Three other young ladies were sitting on the sofa. I stopped and stared at them, unsure what to do next. Miss Clary smiled at me across the room and beckoned me forward. The women on the sofa began to whisper and titter behind their hands as I rattled clumsily towards them, spilling more milk as I went. Miss Hickson, taking pity on me, stepped over and took the tray out of my hands. I curtsied and made to turn away.

'No, no, girl! Stay.' Mistress Lacey laughed. 'We didn't summon you here to fetch us tea. Mrs Mangan really is impossible; she knew I intended *her* to bring up the tray. Never mind – you're here. There's no need for your cap.'

I smiled uncertainly at Miss Hickson as she began to unpin my apron. Miss Clary darted forward and tugged the cap offa my head, allowing my hair to fall about my shoulders.

'May I present ...' Miss Clary turned to the watching women with a flourish of her hand, 'Taney Tyrell!'

The women broke into applause. Applause! I looked at Miss Clary in astonishment but again it was Miss Hickson who came to my aid.

'You are to read our tea leaves,' she whispered, as she drew me towards the women seated about the fire.

The three visitors – the Misses Wilkies, they were called – leaned forward eagerly to examine me.

'So, this is the necklace-finder!'

'Her hair is just as you described it, Clary.'

'She's very young; you never said she was so young.' Their laughter set the china tinkling.

'Well,' Mistress Lacey smiled graciously, 'just as soon as we heard that the Wilkie sisters were to over-winter in the city this year we set to thinking how we could entertain you. Clary suggested we ask our necklace-finder to read our futures for us. I think you will find it very novel, indeed. Prepare to be astonished!'

I squirmed under their scrutiny. Eventually the giggling subsided and I was just standing there, all six women staring at me.

'We sent for you under false pretences, Taney,' Mistress Lacey said. She turned to her guests. 'Her step-mama, I think, would not have let the girl come if she knew she'd be reading our cups, so we had to invent a story about the scullery maid taking ill.'

The women all smiled at her cleverness and nodded, never taking their eyes offa me.

'And my housekeeper was aghast when I ordered up boiled water and cakes for this evening. "Ma'am," she said, "are you quite sure 'tis tea wit cu'cubry san'wiches an' cakes you'll be wantin' at eight of an evenin?" She looked at me as if I were quite mad!'

Her imitation of Missus Mangan set the women giggling again but I could see Mistress Lacey beginning to colour. She seemed at a loss to know how to begin the evening's entertainment and her guests were starting to fidget as they stared at the charwoman's daughter standing in their midst.

'Well? What do we do, girl?' Mistress Lacey asked.

'Drink yer tea,' I said. My voice came out all rough and stroppy. To my surprise they all immediately held their cups out to be filled and Mistress Lacey busied herself measuring out the tea leaves and stirring the teapot. I realised they were all waiting for me to take charge. I pushed down my panic and swallowed hard.

You do it for the Misses Davies all the time, I told myself. This is no differ.

But it was. I'd known the Misses Davies for ever, these women were strangers. I cleared my throat and wiped my hands down my petticoat.

'I will pour, ma'am, if I may,' I said.

Mistress Lacey nodded and slid the pot towards me.

'Now,' I said, trying to sound as confident as I could. 'You must all close your eyes a moment and think of a question to ask the leaves.'

I kept my face solemn and made my movements deliberate. The Misses Davies had shown me all the little rituals my mother performed around a reading. They often said my mother had had a way about her that was special, that watching her read the cups used make their spines tingle. When I went gaming with Billy I had to school my features and hide my thoughts but now it seemed Mistress Lacey wanted me to make a show for her guests.

I remembered how I'd stalled the mistress when we were searching for the necklace, by closing my eyes and waving my arms about to add an air of theatre to my search. I thought of the juggler on Oíche Shamhna, how she set up her tricks for us, starting slow, building till she had us all spellbound.

Could I do that? I wondered. I could try.

Miss Hickson proffered the strainer. I smiled and shook my head, and she laughed at her mistake.

'You must drink all but a little of the liquid,' I said as I poured the tea into the little white cups. 'But, once you're near the end, you must swirl the cup, once, twice, thrice −' they followed my instructions as I spoke '− then drain the remaining water away onto the saucer.

'Who will I start with?' I asked.

'You may begin with Miss Hickson,' Mistress Lacey said. 'Her reading will not take long, I'm sure.'

Miss Hickson held out her cup. It looked as if she'd tried to clump all the leaves together in the bottom to spoil the reading but some leaves had stuck to the rim despite that. I stared at the mess of black. Sure enough patterns and pictures began to emerge, like seeing shapes in clouds.

One tiny clump of leaves looked like a mask; that meant there was a hidden secret. I thought of the letters I'd seen under her pillow the day Mistress Lacey's necklace was robbed. She's trying to hide a sweetheart, I thought.

Some of the leaves looked like the figure of a man. He was tall, I sensed, kind and gentle. A line of dots led away from him, and forked in two directions. One way the fork led to a butterfly — expected happiness — he's urging her to elope but she's hesitating. Why? The other path led to a sword — there would be arguments — and a door lock without a key, which meant there'd be obstacles in the path of their love. I could see the figure of a woman and a small letter L — Mistress Lacey, I guessed. A line of dots ran from her straight to the man. Suddenly it all made sense.

Miss Hickson's sweetheart was Mistress Lacey's kin, her brother. I could just imagine the ructions there'd be iffen the mistress once found out about it; she'd put a stop to it there and then.

I looked up at the governess; she was clutching the arms of her chair as if she feared she might fall out of it. My heart went out to her.

She hopes that, with time, they'll get Mistress Lacey's approval, I thought. She's wrong.

'That which'll make you most happy is just within your reach,' I said carefully. 'But you must take it now or others'll interfere and all will be lost. Take care not to wait too long.'

She started, then laughed to cover her concern.

'My goodness, how very mysterious.' Mistress Lacey raised her eyebrows. 'What secrets are you hiding from us, Miss Hickson?'

'This tassomancy is mainly the art of guess and suggestion,' trilled the eldest Miss Wilkie. 'There is no skill to it, I believe, other than that of the actor.'

I looked at the young woman; I saw the flicker o' spite in her eye.

She thinks Miss Hickson has no right to expect any particular happiness being only one step above a servant, I thought. Silly cow!

'The girl found my necklace, though it was concealed in a cushion; I have good reason to believe she has a talent for fortune telling,' Mistress Lacey said haughtily.

'Oh, oh, I did not mean to offend, I'm sure.' But Miss Wilkie's smile said different. I saw her glance at Miss Clary.

Ah! I felt her bitter jealousy. She sees Miss Clary as a rival, I realised.

I could guess why. Miss Clary was quite a beauty. Miss Wilkie was not.

I bit my lip. This woman means to make little of me so that she may make the Laceys look foolish. Then she'll tell all her posh friends that they are simply not worth bothering about.

Well, I'll not be used that way. Not when Miss Clary and Miss Hickson have been so nice to me.

Before I knew what I was doing I'd reached forward and taken Miss Wilkie's hand in my own. She tried to withdraw it but I held fast and turned her hand palm up.

'You were thrown from a horse an' you twelve,' I said. 'You've never sat upon another since.'

Her sisters gasped. She tried again to pull her hand away.

I peered closer then let her hand drop. I looked straight into her eyes. 'You cried and screamed and made your mother

149

promise to tell your father to shoot that horse.'

Miss Wilkie became flustered. Her sisters were nodding and clearly enjoying her discomfort.

'The pony was very wild and contrary,' Miss Wilkie stuttered.

'Poor Petal wasn't cross,' one sister protested. 'Just a little frisky. You were the ill-tempered one; our parents should not have listened to you.'

'I-I was but a child. I had had a fright ...' Miss Wilkie trailed off, red-faced despite the white powder plastered on her skin.

'Don't fret,' I said kindly. 'Your mama did as you asked but your papa did not.'

The three sisters looked at me in surprise. 'But we heard the shot,' the youngest said. 'I cried all night to think sweet Petal was dead, and all because he'd caused Fanny some bruises and a dirty gown.'

'Your father shot his pistol into the straw, then gave the horse away.'

The eldest Miss Wilkie was most put out now, but asked for her leaves to be read all the same.

Ha! I thought. That'll learn you, Miss High an' Mighty!

But I hid my glee at putting her in her place and I was careful to give her good fortune and a rich husband; this seemed to mollify her well enough.

I read for them all after that, and they hanging on my every word.

Miss Clary, I saw, would have happiness iffen she trusted to her own good nature and sense, and did not allow her mama's ambition to decide all she did. Of course, I dared only tell the first part and keep the last to myself.

Mistress Lacey's leaves were all contradictions. Apples and acorns showed prosperity but a tower in their midst meant she had only found disappointment there. Some cats prowled about – false friends – and there was an iceberg, cold and empty. I could see no clear direction for her future in her cup so I raised my eyes and tried to read her face but she was having none of it. Her smile never faltered but her eyes turned steely and she kept me out. I tussled with her a few moments, then gave her a long life and good health.

She was well pleased. She had brought me here to impress her new acquaintances. Now her guests were full of praise for the novelty of it all, even the eldest Miss Wilkie was saying the evening had been a great success. The mistress pressed a silver coin into my hand. A shilling, one whole shilling what'd usually take me an' Mary Kate a whole day to earn.

Miss Clary jumped up and grabbed a little silver box. She shook it gaily in front of the Miss Wilkies and they giggled and popped pennies onto it, and Miss Clary slid those coins into my hand. A quick glance told me I had almost the makings of another shilling.

Miss Hickson rang for Missus Mangan to take the tea things away. When she came, her face was set like a hatchet and she clattered around collecting the dishes and silver spoons.

'Have you brothers and sisters, Taney?' asked Miss Clary, startling me as I tried to help the crotchety housekeeper.

'One brother, Miss Clary,' I answered.

She placed four Bullrudderie cakes on a plate. 'Wrap these

for Taney to take home, Mrs Mangan, if you'd be so kind,' she said.

The housekeeper stamped down to the basement in front of me. She tipped the four cakes from plate to table.

'Wrap them, indeed,' she said. 'Put them in yer pocket; that'll do you. You may be rewarded for yer witchery in this life, Taney Tyrell, but God will have his say in the next.' She emptied the remaining leaves out of the teapot and put them carefully into a bowl to dry. 'An' now we have ta spare Rob ta walk you home an' all,' she grumped.

'Sure I only live around the corner, Missus Mangan, ma'am,' I said airily. 'There's no need for Rob to leave his duties.' I put on my jacket and shawl and picked up the cakes. I smiled at her, at Rob, who looked disappointed, and 'Cepta, who was eyeing my Bullrudderie cakes. I beamed at them all. Mangy Mangan could be as crabby as she chose; her displeasure couldn't dim my delight. I had near two shilling in my pocket and fancy treats in my fist.

More than that, I had enjoyed performing for the Quality. There was a kind of power in having them all thinking I held their future in my hands. I didn't, of course. I could only see what was going to happen anyway. But when I read their cups it was like they thought I was a magician, bestowing gifts.

It's good as gaming with Billy. I thought, as I skipped to the scullery door. Even better, maybe, 'cause I done it all by myself.

The coins jingle-jangling in my pocket, the crumbly

cakes held careful in my hands, I danced up the steps onto Queen Street, I skipped along the cobbles under the lamplight, to the dark space between the houses that is Thundercut Alley.

22

He's here. The strangler is here.

I can feel his presence. He's in the alley where all is shade, even in the middle of a summer's day. On this January night Thundercut has become a dark tunnel, somewhere to stumble, to creep along, keeping your hands on the wall to feel your way. 'Tis my wee road, I know it well. But he's here, the strangler.

My stomach turns over and I stop at the mouth of the alley, frozen with fear. I stare down, though my eyes can see nowt but black. He's in the turn, the kink in the alley where the shadows close around you so completely you can't see your own fingers. The bit where you imagine the ground may well have disappeared with the sun and every step forward might send you tumbling down an inky hole to the centre of the Earth itself.

He's waiting. He's flexing his fingers. He's heard the coins chink in my pocket. I lay my fingers against it to keep them still. I forget to breathe. From where he is he'll be able to see me, a girl, standing silhouetted against the lamplight on Queen Street. I feel dizzy. My spirit wants to leave my body; it wants to go see who's down there, hiding in the alley. I give in. I close my eyes and slouch against the near wall. I feel myself divide and one part of me begins to slip away. My body starts a slow slide to the ground; I begin to float.

No! Stop it!

I pull myself back; I snap my eyes open. I take a deep breath. I get up, push myself away from the wall, and stumble out of Thundercut Alley, back onto Queen Street.

Now what?

Go home the other way, ninny. Take the long way round. Walk, run, but stay in the lamplight.

I'm shaking now, and I've lost the Bullrudderie cakes, but I start to run, turning right onto King Street, right again onto Smithfield, past the shuttered shop fronts. A rubbish picker starts and looks up from his hunt for smelly treasures amongst the market waste.

'Goodnight, young miss,' he says.

'Goodnight,' I reply, but I don't slow down.

Along the front of Missus Kenny's shop, to the corner of our old Dutch Billy. Now I'm at the other end of Thundercut, my end.

I hesitate. The door to our stairs is just there, just there. I force myself towards it. I turn the handle; I tumble in. I close the door and lean against it, stifling a sob.

He's still out there, in the alley. I can feel his presence. But the impulse to strangle is fading out of him. He's moving away.

I crawl up the stairs.

Da! I think. If I tell Da the strangler's out there in our alley Da'll catch him.

I push open our door. Mary Kate and Jon Jon are fast asleep on the old straw mattress.

Da isn't there.

23

Next day was Sunday. No cattle, no hawkers nor criers, just the peal o' church bells drifting across the square. I lay abed late, tossing and dozing, and Mary Kate let me be. To my surprise, I even heard her tell Jon Jon not to wake me.

'Taney was out workin' last night when you was asleep,' she whispered. 'Quiet now, Master Jon Jon, shush.'

'Shush,' he whispered back. 'Taney's sleepin'. Shush, Mammy, shush.'

When I did get up Mary Kate put a bowl of porridge in front of me and asked me about the night before.

'What did they have you do?' she said.

'Washing-up,' I mumbled through a mouthful of oat mush. I handed her a sixpence.

'Sixpence? That much just for washin' dishes?' She looked at the coin in wonder.

'At short notice and at night,' I protested, shovelling the porridge into me as fast as I could. 'May I go out now?' I asked, standing and grabbing my shawl.

'Are you meetin' Billy?'

'Maybe.'

She hesitated just one breath. 'Go on, then,' she said.

I was desperate to find him. I needed to talk to him, needed to tell him about what'd happened last night in the lane. I'd near given up when I spotted him down on Batchelor's Walk, watching the ships. He jumped when I called his name and barely grunted a greeting. He stayed hunched in his bowl and never bothered to turn his head.

'In one of your black moods again, are you?' I asked, attempting a smile.

'What's it ta you iffen I am?' he said.

'T'is my job to shake you outta it!' I declared. 'That's what friends are for.'

'Stop bein' such a kid,' he growled.

I blinked and hid inside my hair.

What had him so cross? Was it something I'd done?

I stood there a moment pretending to look at the boats. I stole a peek sideways at him; his skin was grey and there was a greasy sweat on his face despite the cold o' the morning. The other beggars in the city always looked sickly and frail. But not Billy. Never Billy.

'Are you all right?' I asked, completely forgetting my own concerns. All the terrible winter ailments that might have got to him, and him sleeping rough every night! 'Are you ill?'

'I'm fine,' he snapped. 'Don't be fussin', will ya?'

He was staring at a fine barque. Two men were climbing its rigging, mending and fixing, moving about on the ropes and yard arms like squirrels. I tried to work out how much time had passed since I'd seen Billy last. Had it really been that long? Was that what had him angry?

'Do you want to be on your own?' I asked unhappily.

He didn't answer and I made to walk away.

'Stay,' he said. He looked straight at me then.

'Jay, Billy. You look terrible.' I couldn't stop myself saying it; his eyes were in the back of his head, all bloodshot with big black circles under them.

He shrugged. To my dismay his hands began to tremble and his dark eyes filled with tears.

'I'm in trouble, Taney,' he said. 'Bad trouble.' He wrapped his arms tight around himself, jamming his fingers under his armpits. 'I've been a right fool.' He began to rock forwards and back.

'Jay, Billy.'

'I've been playin' at cards with the Ormond Boys,' he said, so low I had to crouch down to hear him. 'Been losin'. Been losin' bad.'

'How bad?'

'Real bad. They let me play on tick an' now I owe them.'

I caught my breath. The Ormond Market butcher boys were not to be messed with. Everyone knew that. 'How much?'

'More than I can beg.' He began to cough; it turned into a spasm. I hid my concern and didn't remark it, just waited for it to pass. 'More than I can beg in a month o' Sundays,' he said when he could speak again.

'But you said you sometimes make as much as a shilling outside the church door of a Sunday,' I exclaimed.

He shook his head. 'I was boastin', wasn't I? I make sixpence if I'm lucky. This mornin' I made tuppence all told.

A couple o' the Ormond Boys was waiting around the corner for me and they took it offa me straightaway. They said it'd just clear the interest on what they'd loaned me an' I still owed them all the rest. They threatened a beatin' iffen I don't get them at least half what I borrowed by Wednesday next.'

'How much d'you owe them, Billy?' I asked slowly. 'How much all told?'

'More than tuppence.' He began to rock again. 'I was wonderin', Taney, I was wonderin' ... would you come gamin' with me again? Just a few times, till I'm quits with them boyos?'

I breathed in sharp. To my surprise the thought of hanging around the back of inns again and brushing against the drunks and thugs at the old brick field pits made me recoil. I found myself comparing it with last night, dainty teacups held in dainty hands.

'I can't, Billy. Mary Kate and Da won't let me out after dark for a while more yet.' Which were true enough but I turned my face away so as Billy wouldn't see how glad I was of the excuse.

'Sometimes there's a Hazard game out back o' Half Moon on Sundays,' he said eagerly. 'It'd be startin' about now.'

I could feel his eyes on me but I kept my face averted. I could feel a pink flush of guilt creeping across my skin. Did I really care more for fancy china than for Billy? What sort of friend was I?

'Gaming on a Sunday?' I shook my head. 'Mary Kate'd murder me altogether.' I tried to laugh but the desperation I saw on Billy's face when I looked up shook me. I wanted to help him, I really did. But I couldn't go gaming again. I just couldn't. I was done with all that; it seemed a low kind of life to me now. I wanted something better.

It's not wrong to want something better for myself, it's not. But Billy's face.

I remembered my locking box. All that money I'd saved. I took a deep breath. Billy was my best friend. He had rescued me once; now it was my turn to rescue him.

'I have about six shilling. I'll give it you gladly.'

He looked up at me, all astonishment. 'Six shillin'?'

'The winnings I've saved and two shilling I got last night.' I beamed at him, then faltered. 'Well, I had to give Mary Kate sixpence this morning so it's only five an' six.'

'But that's near enough what I need.' Billy's eyes had brightened and he'd stopped the awful rocking. 'How'd you get two whole shillin' last night? Did you find it on road or what?'

'I earned it,' I said, relieved to see that old blackness shifting.

'How?' He looked at me queer. 'Have ya been playin' Hazard without me, Taney Tyrell?'

'No, I haven't. Are you daft? No one would let a kid like me in on a game.' I grinned, and told him about the night before at Number Eleven and reading their tea leaves. He laughed to hear of the eldest Miss Wilkie's embarrassment and was interested to know that Mistress Lacey was able to hide her future from me.

'So you can't always see what folk are up to?' He smiled a proper smile at last, one that reached his eyes and set his dimples dancing.

161

'I used to only be able to see whatever popped into my head – you know that. Now, if I concentrate hard on someone, I can usually see something about them, something from their past or future. But iffen they know I'm looking, and they're really determined to stop me, there's a few folk can hide things. I can never see anything much for Da nor Mary Kate, for instance,' I said. I bit my lip. 'Something else happened last night, though, Billy. Something bad.'

He looked at me. 'Well?' he said, when I stayed silent.

'When it happened before I promised Da I wouldn't tell no one.' I heard the shake in my voice as I spoke and Billy frowned. 'But I've got to; iffen I have to hold it in any longer I'll burst, I will.'

'What is it? What's happened?'

I sat down beside him and told him it all. I told him about the strangler in the alley the night before. And then I told him of the night I floated and saw the attack on Barrack Street.

Billy looked horrified. 'But you didn't see the strangler's face?'

'No, I never.'

'An' you told no one else?'

'Da and Mary Kate know about the first time; Da made me swear I'd say nothing. He said folk'd just think I was looking for attention.'

Billy shook his head. 'He's afeard o' more than that, you goose.' His voice was sharp; I stared at him. 'What d'you think the strangler would do iffen he heard there was someone who'd witnessed what he'd done? D'ya think he'd take a chance on it bein' true you hadn't seen him proper?'

I felt the blood drain from my face.

'Yer da's right, Taney.' Billy's voice was urgent. 'You have ta promise me like ya promised him. You mustn't tell another soul what you seen. Promise me.'

I nodded. I was a goose an' all, not to have realised the danger of seeing what I saw. How could I have been so stupid?

'An' iffen that's what you see when you go floatin' you should stop doin' it, like yer da says.'

I nodded again.

'Promise?'

'I promise.'

We watched the ships a few moments more but I wasn't really looking at them, just waiting for my heart to go back to normal. What if the strangler did find out I'd seen him? Da and Billy were right. I must be more careful of who knew what. But Billy'd never tell no one. Billy'd look out for me.

'Taney ...' Billy cleared his throat. 'I wonder could we ...' He let the sentence dangle and turned a bit pink in the face.

I scrambled to my feet. 'Of course. I'm sorry, Billy. Sooner you pay that debt the better. Come on home with me and I'll fetch the money down from my locking box.'

He turned bright red. ''Tis yer runnin' away money yer givin' me,' he said, slumping in his bowl. 'Yer sure about it?'

'O' course I am,' I said stoutly, though, truth told, I knew 'twas going to give me more than a pang to take all them coins from my mother's box.

But when are you going to run, Taney Tyrell? I asked myself. No time soon. Billy needs that money now. Iffen you're not going gaming with him then 'tis the least you can do for your friend, and him in trouble.

'Yer a star, Taney Tyrell,' Billy said, as he began to turn his bowl. 'Yer the best.'

The colour was back in his cheeks and he shook his hair offa his face. He looked like his handsome self again. 'Twas me had put the smile back on his face. Me. Them pangs at giving him my running away money were nothing to the flush o' pride I felt as we set off along the quays. I loved being with him. I loved being seen with him.

I wasn't afraid now neither. Not of stranglers nor Pinkindindies nor Ormond Boys. It was the middle of the day and besides, Billy was with me.

24

The local kids had taken over the square. Some were kicking a pig's bladder about and some more had marked the ground for hopscotch; groups of girls were skipping rope; a boy was chasing a hoop. But even with the skipping songs and the shouts of the ball players, Smithfield was quiet of a Sunday afternoon.

As I dropped the coins into Billy's hand I spotted Mary Kate and Jon Jon coming across the market square. The sharp clack of Mary Kate's heels on the cobbles told me that this morning's good humour was gone.

'Yer step-mam looks like she has a right bee in her bonnet,' Billy said, pocketing the coins. 'I'll be off.' He put his batons to the ground and turned to go. 'Thanks, Taney. You've saved me skin, you have. I owe you.'

'You're my best friend, Billy,' I said, feeling awkward. 'You don't owe me nowt.'

By the time Mary Kate and Jon Jon reached me, Billy was t'other side of the square, disappearing up Duck Lane. Jon Jon threw himself into my arms like he hadn't seen me for days.

'Taney, Taney, Taney,' he yelled. 'Play with me, Taney. Play chase.'

Mary Kate jerked him away and looked around her. Jenna Mooney was coming out of Thundercut, herding the three littlest Mooneys, all sticky and snotty, in front of her.

'Will you mind Jon Jon a minute, Jenna?' Mary Kate asked. 'Taney and me need to talk.' Jenna nodded and Mary Kate pushed Jon Jon towards the little group. 'They'll play chase with you, lovey,' she said as she turned back to me, folding her arms across her chest as she did so.

'I met Missus Mangan this mornin',' she said. 'You've got some explainin' to do.'

I considered turning tail and scarpering but I knew that'd only make things worse. Mary Kate wouldn't holler after me, she wouldn't make a show of me, but she'd keep all her anger simmering till I came home, even if I waited till midnight. I stayed put and stared at my shoes.

'Mangy Mangan should mind her own business,' I muttered.

'We need that job in Queen Street, Taney.' Mary Kate kept her voice low, though no one could hear her anyways. 'I'll not have your so-called gift spoilin' that for us, d'you hear?'

"Twas you told them I read the leaves,' I protested.

'Not so as you'd go readin' for them,' she snapped.

'But they were delighted with me,' I said. 'They paid me well.'

'This time. What if they hadn't liked what you told them? Them sort turn quick. One minute you're their darlin' an' can do no wrong, next you're dirt on their foot and they can't wait to shake you off.'

'What was I supposed to do, then?' I bridled at her. 'Refuse to do what they wanted?'

'You should have! You should have made some excuse, said you couldn't do it. Iffen I'd a known what they wanted you for I'd have said you was sick. No good can come from your tellin' folk things that haven't happened yet. 'Tisn't right.'

'You never said that when they give me the taffety gown,' I said.

'I should never have let you accept it. God forgive me for bein' so weak-minded.' She shook her head. 'We can't afford to lose this work, I tell you. With your da outta work, we're barely able to get by.'

'You were happy enough to take the money I got this morning.'

'That was before. I didn't know it was tainted, then.'

'Tainted? Like me?'

'Tainted, like your witch of a mother,' she snapped.

I swallowed hard. This wasn't fair; it wasn't fair at all.

'You're just jealous,' I snarled. 'Da loved my mother more than he'll ever love you and you can't stand that, can you?'

She snorted. 'Your da may have loved her once but by the end he fair hated her, an' that's the truth of it.' She spat the words out, her face a picture of scorn.

I stared at her. She caught her breath and her hand flew to her mouth, too late to stop her words.

'I didn't mean it,' she said. 'I didn't. It's not true.'

But she knew, and I knew, that she wasn't inclined to telling lies.

I stumbled backwards.

'I hate you,' I said. 'I hate you like I've never hated anyone, ever.'

I turned and ran across the square, through the hopscotch and around the skipping, into Duck Lane, running to find Billy.

Billy'd listen. Billy'd understand.

25

I lurched past the shabby little shops all shuttered up. I couldn't hardly see for the tears in my eyes, and the anger was so hot inside me I couldn't hardly breathe neither. I skirted a heap of slops and tripped over the legs of a dozing drunk.

'Watch where yer goin', dunderhead!' he growled.

'Excuse me, sir, but have you seen Billy-the-bowl, sir?' I asked.

'What's it to you iffen I have?'

'He's my friend; I need to find him. Did you see which way he went?' I asked. 'This or that?' I pointed either direction on Bow Street.

'That,' he said, without looking up or pointing.

'Which way is that?' I asked again.

'That way, that way, ya ninny!' He jerked his head slightly to the left. I thanked him and turned up the street.

At the junction with King Street a woman was selling posies.

'For yer sweetheart, the one you fancy, Bridget, Mary, Ann or Nancy,' she called to some young men passing.

'Excuse me, but have you seen Billy-the-bowl?' I asked her.

She smiled. 'He went up to Old Church Street and turned

off at the Watch Tower. I think he was headed towards Brunswick Street.'

At the top o' Brunswick Street I asked some kids. They took my hand and pulled me back along the road to the turn for Grange Gorman Lane.

'Dat way, missy,' they said.

'Are you sure?' I asked.

They nodded. I looked up towards The Half Moon winking at me in the winter sun.

No.

No, he never.

I couldn't move.

'Dat's where Billy-bowl went, missy,' said the smallest boy, tugging at my petticoat. 'We tolt ya true. D'ya not be beliefin' us?'

He's paying off his debts, you eejit, I thought, shaking off the boy's hand. That's all Billy's doing; he's paying his debts.

But iffen he knew he was headed here when he left me why didn't he leave Smithfield Square by King Street and come straightest road? Why go all about the houses? An' why didn't he say that he was headed to The Half Moon, unless he didn't want me to know?

I started up the lane, slowly at first, for my legs felt like lead. My head was getting all hot, boiling with rage at Mary Kate and questions for Billy, everything jumbled into one big angry blur.

I broke into a jog.

I rounded the inn at a run and came into the yard so fast I near tripped over Matt Davern's terrier. It jumped up, giving one sharp yap. The circle of watchers turned around. Matt Davern's head appeared above them, looking to see what had set his dog off.

'Come to help young Billy out, Taney?' Matt asked, grinning at me. 'Yer his good luck charm, you are; don't win half so much when yer not wi' him.'

The watchers laughed at Matt's wee joke, though Matt suddenly seemed struck by what he'd just said. He stood staring at me; I could see his face working as his brain slowly gathered up old memories and put them with new. Everyone else had turned back to the game.

I ignored Matt's accusing eyes and stepped forward, pushing between two watchers. Five men were squatting on the ground and there in the middle of them was Billy, looking up at me, horrified, one hand cupped around the dice, the other laying down a coin. A King George ha'penny. My ha'penny.

'Taney,' he stuttered, lost for words this once.

I felt the tears start to my eyes. I swiped at them angrily with one hand. 'Go to hell, Billy,' I shouted. 'Go to hell.'

'What's up with her?' and 'Never mind the young wan, get on wi' the game,' is all I heard as I ran from the yard of The Half Moon Inn. I kept on running till I was back at the junction of Grange Gorman and Brunswick Street.

I looked back up the lane.

In my mind's eye I saw dice roll in the dirt.

26

I turned fourteen in February. There was no money at home to spare for treats or gifts that year. The Misses Davies gave me a handkerchief with lace in one corner; Missus Kenny gave me an old pair of pattens to save my shoes in bad weather.

I hadn't seen sight nor sign of Billy since that day he'd gone and gambled my running-away money. I hadn't seen him and I hadn't looked for him neither. I was full of anger with him for what he'd done. But I missed him all the same, and that made me angry with myself.

Only a fool misses him what betrayed her, I told myself furiously. Forget him. He used you.

Somewhere in the back of my mind lurked the awful thought that maybe that's all he'd ever been doing. Maybe, for Billy, our friendship had only ever been about winning pennies. No. That couldn't be true. The thought of that near made me sick.

I put my lace hankie away safe in my locking box. It was the only thing of value in there; all my money was gone. Iffen I'd had that money now I'd have run away to London for sure. Mary Kate and me only spoke to each other if we had to; I couldn't forget what she'd said about Da hating my mother and I couldn't forgive her for believing it was true. Being out of work all this time was getting to Da. He used only go for a drink with his friends one evening a week. Now, despite how little money was coming into the house, he was staying out near every night. He was silent and sour most days. Even Jon Jon caught the bad atmosphere in the attic and became whingey-whiney.

It rained and rained that spring. Every day was grey and the streets were soaked. Missus Kenny's pattens kept me out of the worst of it, though they were the very divil to walk in. I kept my petticoats pinned up whenever I was out, even so mud splashed up from coaches, water sloshed down from pipes and eaves and it was impossible to go out without getting filthy wet.

Fourteen, it seemed to me, was dull and coloured grey-brown.

March dripped by and April came in cold and damp. My only joy was my days at Number Eleven. The Wilkie sisters had told all their fancy friends of the unusual entertainment they had had at the house on Queen Street and now Mistress Lacey and Miss Clary were preparing to host an evening for twenty women from the best families Dublin city had to offer. There was to be a rustic theme with the guests to come dressed as milkmaids and country girls. A peasant feast of oysters, coddle and soda bread was to be laid on, and local musicians would play country airs. But the main entertainment of the night was me, for I was to tell all the young ladies' fortunes.

Such a thing was not to be planned quickly, it seemed. Mistress Lacey decided it couldn't be held till the parlours had had a new coat of paint in a more fashionable colour. Some new chairs must be purchased to seat all the guests, and the carpets and drapes were to be taken outside and cleaned. The date set for it was the first week of May, more than a month away, when the days would be longer and the weather more clement. Invitations were written and sent out.

Mary Kate knew all about it and Da did too, but there was nowt they could say nor do to stop it without endangering our working there. To add to Mary Kate's annoyance, every time we arrived at Number Eleven I'd be pulled away by Miss Clary to hear all the latest ideas and plans.

'We won't keep her long, Mary Kate,' Miss Clary'd promise, as she beckoned me up to Miss Hickson's attic room.

There they would show me drawings of the costumes we were to wear, they'd talk of the decorations planned for the parlours, they'd gossip about the intended guests. I was that excited by it all I didn't say much, just smiled and nodded, loving being welcomed into their world of lace and fine shiny things. Every now and then Miss Clary would make a coy remark about her governess' mystery beau and Miss Hickson would blush, and shush her.

'Well, there's no point trying to hide your secrets from Taney,' Miss Clary would say with a laugh. 'She knows your own heart better than you do, don't you, Taney?'

I'd giggle and shake my head, and Miss Hickson'd change the subject, which'd make her pupil tease her all the more. How I loved being in on their plans. It all seemed a thousand miles away from the grubby games out back of The Half Moon. When I was with Miss Clary and Miss Hickson

I could almost forget how much I missed Billy. By the time I'd return to Mary Kate most of our chores would be done and Mary Kate'd be cross as a briar. I didn't care two straws for that.

Mistress Lacey was treating me like I was special too, asking my opinion on the teacups and the best sort of tea to use. I knew she was only being nice to me because I was of use to her, but somehow this party felt like it was mine. I was at its very centre. I was cast as lead actress and the front parlour would be my stage.

Down in the kitchen no one was speaking to me at all. Missus Mangan refused to even notice I was in the room and 'Cepta and Rob were too scared of her not to follow her example. All talk'd stop as soon as I walked in and the whispering would begin as I left. Didn't care 'bout that neither. The kitchen prattle was only about the latest victims of the Stoneybatter Strangler anyways. There'd been two more girls attacked, one near the Linen Hall and one on Montpelier Hill. Both had survived; neither had been able to give a description of their attacker. They'd each lost their week's wages — four, five shilling a piece. But ever since Billy had pointed out the danger of having witnessed the first strangling I had decided to block out all thoughts of the Stoneybatter Strangler and the dreadful thing I'd witnessed. I shut my ears. I shut my mind, and iffen those being strangled had called my spirit to float, I never knew nowt of it, thanks be.

Mistress Lacey had promised me five whole shillings as payment for my role in her rustic evening *and* whatever her guests chose to put in my palm on the night besides. I reckoned

175

I might earn as much as eight shilling all told, maybe even ten. It would go straight into my locking box, as much of it as I could hide from Mary Kate.

Every night since Billy had lost my running away money I opened the box and looked at the place where it had been. I would start again. I would earn all this money on my own; I didn't need Billy Bowl to help me. Now I didn't have Billy I had no reason to stay here. I would go to London some day, like I'd always said I would.

Some day soon.

27

I'm back in the yard of The Half Moon. There's light inside the pub; I can see silhouettes of drinkers inside the windows; someone has started a song. The yard is empty, 'cept for a scrawny cat prowling; it don't pay me no heed as I drift about the yard. There *is* a half moon and all – well near enough half anyways – up in the sky. By the light of it I can see the marks in the dirt where folk gather to watch the Hazard games and the flat bit in the middle where the men play.

There Billy sat, I think. There he rolled the dice. There he played all my money, my money that I gave him in friendship 'cause I believed he was in trouble.

In the last couple of weeks I've taken to coming here near every night, floating. I know I promised Da I wouldn't float iffen I could help it but Da doesn't seem to care much what I do these days. He hardly seems to know I'm there. So at night I put my hand down to my mother's locking box and trace the flowers with my finger.

Mother, I think. Look at me. I'm doing what you used do.

I can do it at will now. I just open my mind and let the whole world rush in at once. I've learned not to panic, not to fight it. I've learned not to connect with them voices, their wants and their hurts. I just let them pass through; I never let them call my spirit to them and their troubles. The din is horrendous. My head feels fit to burst and my stomach lurches. Then all goes quiet and I am free to go where I choose. Tonight I look down at my freckled face unconscious in my window bed.

Billy Bowl's a liar, I think. The dandies on Dame Street'll never be falling at your feet, Taney girl. This is your gift. This.

And away I float.

I've fallen in love with the night, with the darkness. I can feel the cold but it doesn't bother me. Everything is more than itself when I float. Sharper. Clearer.

And yet, everything is less. Nothing can hurt me up here. I pass over people and their pain. I see it, know it, but it doesn't touch me. I float high. Over the roofs, above the trees, through clouds. The night wraps around me like a silky shadow. It whispers in my ear, inviting me to fly higher, fly straight offa the world and touch the stars.

I want to.

Some night I will.

But each night I break free of its embrace and float down to The Half Moon.

All day, every day, I push down my anger at Billy. All day long I convince myself that I don't miss him an' he such a false friend, yet here I am again at The Half Moon, where I last seen him. Maybe iffen I come often enough I'll understand how he could do such a thing to me.

I recall his face the morning we watched the ships – his

grey pallor, how he rocked back and forth. I was so worried about him that day, thinking how hard life on the streets must be on a body, terrified to see him sickening like that.

But I can't forgive him. He lied to me, used me.

Go home, you ninny, I tell myself.

I should be home in bed with the rest of me but every night I am more reluctant to end my night wanders. I like hovering above the street, watching folk. I float out of the yard, into the lane. At the far end of it I make out a girl kissing her sweetheart goodnight.

But is he a false lad or a true? I ask the night. The night doesn't answer so I float down closer so to see for myself.

The lad has a bonny smile. He wants to walk the girl all the way to her door but she's laughing and pointing up the lane.

'Sure I'm nearly there,' she says. 'Go on with ya. Go off home ta yer bed and I'll be off home ta mine.'

He gives her sixpence from his week's wages. They've been saving for months; she keeps their money in a jar.

'It won't be long till we have enough to marry on,' she says. They embrace again and part. She waves over her shoulder as she turns up towards The Half Moon. She's smiling as she walks. She twirls her bonnet in her hand.

But someone's watching her, someone else than me. He's up ahead in the shadows. He flexes his fingers. He's wearing gloves this time. Despite the fear that's begun to crawl about me I think to float towards him, to look at his face, to see who it is that's half-strangling and robbing the servant girls of Stoneybatter.

179

It's nowt to do with you, I scold myself. Stay outta it. Go home to bed.

I make to go but the fear inside me suddenly twists to terror and I can't ignore it. I remember Hallowe'en night, months ago now. I see the fire in the eyes of the skulls. I remember what them eyes told me.

In a few moments the girl will be up at the part of the road where the strangler is hid. If he once catches hold of her, if he wraps his hands around her neck, I know, know it to my very marrow, that girl will never marry her lad.

28

I woke up with a start. I gripped the blanket tight about me.

There's nowt you can do, it's none of your business, I told myself, squeezing my eyes tight shut. But all I could see inside my head was the girl, kissing her lad and dreaming of their future.

Oh god, oh god, she's going to die, I thought. Iffen I do nowt she has no future.

I sat up quietly and began pulling on my clothes, grabbing my shoes. I sneaked out of the attic, trying not to let the door handle groan. I felt my way down the stairs, stepping quick and careful around all the old creaks. Once I was through the door and out in the alley, I ran. I didn't worry 'bout tripping or puddles; nowt mattered if I could just get to the lane in time. I was afraid that by now the strangler's hands were already on the girl's neck and she was fighting him.

He doesn't mean to kill, I thought. He's after her money, is all. But she's fighting too hard; she's not passing out like the servant girl in Barrack Street.

The moon had slipped behind a cloud; Brunswick Street was dark. I tried not to slow down but the horror of what

I could see in my mind's eye was turning my legs to water.

He's panicking, I thought. He's squeezing her neck harder. Her eyes are glazing over.

'Stop it!' I yelled. 'Stop!'

I was in the lane but I was too late. Somewhere up ahead of me in the dark she was drawing her last breath. I sank down to the ground, desperate tears blurring my eyes. I held myself tight. The silence was awful.

Then twigs crunching and breaking.

Him scarpering into the bushes, I guessed.

I was at one end of the lane, shaking and sobbing; the girl was at the other end, growing cold. The cloud passed offa the moon but it was a while before I could bring myself to stand up and creep along the road to where I knew she'd be.

Her bonnet was rolling in the dirt. Her eyes were staring at me. I turned away. I saw something black in the dark of the ditch. I crept closer. A glove, two gloves, their fingers all twisted and inside out where he'd peeled them off and flung them there. I backed away, stumbling and heaving till I was back down on Brunswick Street again. I vomited on the mill wall.

'What the blazes?' A voice boomed out in the dark. I swung around, petrified.

'Taney?' Da was staring at me like he couldn't believe his eyes. 'What in God's name are ya doin' here?'

'Da, Da, Da,' I groaned, and fell into his arms. 'She's dead, Da, he's killed her, Da.'

'Who? Who killed who?' His eyes followed my pointing finger but the girl was too far up the lane for him to see her.

'What's happened, Taney? What have you seen?'

I tried to tell him about floating and seeing the girl. About knowing she would die and trying to reach her in time. About being too late. It all came out garbled and jagged and Da just stood there looking at me, horrorstruck.

I tried to tug him up the lane to show her to him, thinking that he would make it all right. Maybe she wasn't quite dead. Maybe he'd know how to make her breathe again.

But Da wouldn't come with me up the lane.

'The last stragglers will be out o' The Half Moon in a bit,' he said, his voice low now. 'They'll find her. They'll sound the alarm. You an' me are goin' home. We're gettin' out o' this place afore anyone sees us.'

He pulled me away.

When we reached Thundercut he put his hand on my shoulder and turned my face to his.

'I know nothing I say means aught to you no more—'

I began to shake my head in protest but he shushed me. 'Yer tellin' fortunes for the Quality despite knowin' how me an' Mary Kate feel 'bout it. Yer goin' yer own way an' I can't stop you but you'll heed this one thing, Taney.' His eyes were cold and his fingers bit into my chin. 'You'll say nothin' about this to no one. Ever.' He shook me once, like folk shake a spider from a shoe. 'Not even to me. D'ya hear? I mean to forget this ever happened. You'll do the same. 'Tis nowt to do with ya. Nowt.'

He opened the door and pushed me in ahead of him. He looked around the alley before he closed the door, like he was checking no one had seen us.

My legs were gone from under me. I went up them stairs half on my hands and knees. I didn't bother to take off my dress, just crawled under my blanket and curled up, digging my fingers into my arms as I held them tightly 'round me.

I never slept that night. If I closed my eyes I'd see things I didn't want to see. The girl's eyes staring. Her bonnet rolling. And when dawn came, Da's hands on my shoulder and chin. And he's not wearing his gloves, the gloves I got him with the taffety gown.

29

'I always lock the front door of an evenin', Miss Ruth, you know that,' Missus Kenny said, batting Horace away from the milk jug. 'An' I've axed Mary Kate to lock the lane door at seven bells. The strangler'll not come into this house iffen Jane Kenny has anything to say about it.'

Miss Ruth nodded and tried to smile but her teacup was rattling in her hand so much she had to set it down. Miss Evelyn patted her sister's shoulder but I could tell she was upset herself. The news of the murder was all over the city. No one had talked about anything else for the last three days.

'And they say the poor girl was to be married soon, to a very nice young man,' Miss Ruth said, fidgeting with her hankie. 'I'm sure his heart is broken, poor boy.' Her voice gave and she buried her face in the white linen.

I was dusting and cleaning and trying to block it all out. Jittery as a mouse, I'd been, ever since that night in the lane. The last few days were spent keeping myself too busy to think and falling onto my bed at night only to find my sleep laced with nightmares. My head was full of the girl's eyes, the gloved hands.

Da was still going out of a night, drinking with his pals.

He was always in bad humour afterwards and he smelled strange. It musta been the beer. He was hiding something from me, I could sense it. In my heart I couldn't believe he had aught to do with that girl's death and I didn't want to know, iffen he had. But what was Da doing over on Brunswick Street that night? He usually drank in The Swan, at the other end of Smithfield.

He'd hardly spoke a word to me since. I wondered if this was how things had gone with my mother, him growing cold and distant when she didn't give up using her gifts. Is this what Mary Kate meant when she claimed he had hated my mam in the end? I was losing Da because of my gifts. I'd lost Billy despite them.

Gifts! Curses, more like. I was being forced to see terrible things, things that made my stomach churn each time I thought of them. I longed to leave Smithfield, leave Dublin, leave everything I knew behind, start my life again somewhere far away. Only the excitement of the party at Number Eleven cut through the bleakness of the days.

'Is it true the girl was only seventeen, Missus Kenny?' Miss Evelyn was asking now.

I leaned my forehead against the bookcase and closed my eyes.

I wish I could close my ears an' all, I thought. I wish to God they'd change the subject.

'Did I tell you about the evening Mistress Lacey and Miss Clary are planning, Miss Ruth?' I said, turning around and forcing a smile.

'You did, but tell us again,' Missus Kenny said, winking

at me. 'Let's talk o' something more cheerful, for no amount o' ullagonin' will bring that poor lass back now.'

'They're having a gay coloured gown made for me. I'm to be got up like a gypsy, with a silk scarf tied around my head and big hooped earrings.' I pranced around the Misses Davies' parlour, swirling my petticoat out. 'And there's to be a tent, all hung about with ribbons, a little tent in which I'll sit and tell the ladies' fortunes.'

Miss Ruth dabbed her nose and tried to smile.

'This is how I shall make a living,' I announced, stopping suddenly in mid-twirl. My skirt flopped around my legs. 'I'll go to London and tell fortunes for the Quality! I'll earn ten shillings every week! I'll have all the frippery I choose and eat gingerbread every day!'

Missus Kenny cackled and exchanged a knowing look with Miss Evelyn.

'And why shouldn't I?' I demanded, annoyed. 'The Quality like me, so they do. They like to have their future told just like you and the Misses Davies.'

Missus Kenny cocked an eyebrow. 'The folk on Queen Street aren't no differ to you an' me in most things, I'll give you that. They have ta eat. They have ta sleep. They have ta piddle in a pot.' She laughed. 'But they eat offa china, sleep on feathers, an' the pots what they piddle in are made o' china an' all.'

'A tent, all hung about with ribbons,' Miss Ruth said dreamily, staring out the window.

'I'm sure it will be lovely, dear,' Miss Evelyn said. 'But Taney must be careful not to get too carried away. You and

I know only too well how fickle the so-called Quality can be.'
Miss Evelyn pressed her lips together. 'They will play with
you as long as you amuse them and cast you off when they are
done with you, my dear,' she said to me.

'That's what Mary Kate says.' I was tired of everyone being
against me. I felt my face set into a sulk. 'They're being nice
to me an' I'm having fun. Why can't folk just be happy for
me?'

Missus Kenny raised an eyebrow. 'We're happy for you,
Taney. We're just sayin' don't go settin' yer heart on it
happenin' more 'en once or twice, is all. Them folk is all 'bout
money an' status, an' you don't have neither. They've taken a
fancy to yer gift an' what it can do for them. The Laceys have
some money but 'tis new money an' that don't count much
with the nobility. Clarissa Lacey will inherit a decent fortune
an' she has a pretty face, I hear. 'Tis said her mam has her
sights set on marryin' her off to a title.'

'Then her mama will need to throw her daughter in the
way of the older families,' Miss Evelyn said.

'An' she knows right well iffen she sent invites to a gaggle
o' uppercrust ladies just for dinner or afternoon tea, they'd
send back their apologies, every one,' Missus Kenny said,
watching Horace make another advance on the milk jug. 'So
she arranges an evenin' so unusual they can't resist it! She's a
clever one, all right.' Missus Kenny rapped the cat sharpish
on the nose and pushed him offa the table. Miss Ruth fluttered
anxiously. 'Them Laceys are posh but not posh enough for
the old families to take much notice of.' Missus Kenny
addressed this last to me.

'So, the Laceys are using me. So what?' I said, stung by the thought though I knew it was true. 'What's it to me? I'll use them right back. And anyway, I know Miss Clary likes me. She's always nice to me, she is.'

'Just have a care, Taney,' Miss Evelyn said as firmly as she could manage. 'The women you'll meet are spoiled and used to having their way in all things. Many of them are quite good-hearted, I'm sure. But . . .' she hesitated, 'they are women and their futures are uncertain. Much will depend on whom they marry. You need to have a care what fortunes you foretell for them. Even Clarissa Lacey, for all her father's money, will depend for her happiness on the man her parents choose for her.'

I snorted. 'Iffen she doesn't like him, she can always leave him.'

'She can,' Missus Kenny said, tilting her head to one side and regarding me from under raised eyebrows. 'But iffen she leaves him she leaves her money with him an' every bit o' respectability she ever had as well.'

'Women shouldn't marry at all, so,' I said, shrugging.

'If a girl doesn't marry and has no fortune of her own she must depend completely on the kindness of her family,' Miss Evelyn said softly. 'Our dear papa left us this house but no income on which to live. He expected our brother, James, to provide us with support, but James has five children living and considers us well enough looked after.'

'This was your house?' I was astonished.

'It was once our family's town residence,' Miss Evelyn said.

'James has a finer house now in Fitzwilliam Square, as well as the family estate in Kildare.'

'But how come Missus Kenny owns your house?' I asked.

'Missus Kenny purchased the house from us five years after we inherited it, and agreed my sister and I should live on this floor for as long as we wish to,' Miss Evelyn said. 'That way we continue to live in this familiar house and have enough money to live on.' Miss Evelyn had turned rosy pink but seemed determined to tell me how things were for her and Miss Ruth. 'Living simply in a lodging house puts us beyond the friendship of our former acquaintances. We were dropped by nearly all of them shortly after our father died.'

'There, there, Miss Ruth, don't go upsettin' yerself.' Missus Kenny bustled over to Miss Ruth who had begun to cry again. 'Folk like that aren't worth spillin' tears over. Aren't you surrounded be yer friends here? Yer sister? Me an' Taney an' Milo an' Mary Kate an' wee Jon Jon? Horace?'

Miss Ruth nodded and tried to smile but I could see her mind was away in a world where folk had parties and balls and evenings with coloured tents and dangling ribbons. I bit my lip, ashamed. My old friends had distressed themselves in order that I might understand more of the way o' the world.

But that's not how it'll be for me, I thought. I won't depend on some man to provide for me. I won't depend on anyone. I *will* go to London an' I *will* make my fortune there.

I looked down at the square. It was horse market day, my favourite fair day, for the rest was mostly cows, cows, sheep and cows. I loved horses, and I knew Miss Ruth did too.

190

'The fair's in full swing now, Miss Ruth,' I said, bringing her attention to the window.

Missus Kenny linked her arm in Miss Ruth's and walked her over. Hundreds of horses were standing below us, snorting, whinnying, shifting from hoof to hoof, their breath visible in the sharp morning air. Most stood easy; some skittish ones were tossing their heads about and backing up, yanking on their ropes. Farmers leaning on sticks and chawing on pipes were touching the brims of their hats in greeting to each other and barking orders to the eager young lads holding the ropes. This end of the square was full of piebalds and skewbalds. I could see one long string of docile white ponies with long creamy manes and brown spots on their rumps.

'Oh, look,' Miss Ruth cooed, pointing to a Connemara pony just below the window, being minded by a child of no more than five.

'Is it a horse you've got there or a dog, wee man?' Missus Kenny stuck her head outta the window and bellowed down to the boy below. He turned his head upwards and stuck out his tongue, which only made her laugh the more.

At the other end of the square the finest of the horses were gathered – stallions, nervous and beautiful, and fine mares, greys and bays, chestnuts, roans and black. Young squires and their grooms strolled about looking these over and making deals with the farmers. At the far side of the square lads raced horses up and down, riding bareback.

'Oh!' Miss Evelyn exclaimed. 'How lovely!' Another horse was being led into the square, a smoky grey with white stars scattered all over its rump, and a mane and tail of pure white. It looked, I thought, like it had been moonstruck. Everyone in the square was turning to stare at it as it was led into the centre. The man leading the moon horse brought it to a stand. Horses and folk shifted around it. The moon horse took a step backwards. And there was Billy.

I started. I hadn't seen him in so long. He had settled himself midway along a kind of path that served as a crossway through the market for those what didn't want to weave amongst the horses. In the window glass I saw my reflection flinch; a sour look that'd rival the worst of Mary Kate's came over my face. I closed my eyes and turned away.

They're coming for him.

The thought came out of nowhere.

The House of Industry men were coming for Billy. I could see them in my mind's eye.

They're in Red Cow Lane, I thought. They're after him. They mean to catch him and bring him in.

I turned back to the window.

What do I care what happens to him? I thought bitterly. He's no friend o' mine. Let him fend for himself.

But them men, they have a piece of paper what gives them the right to take him. They'll lock him up, like they did when he was little. They have a House of Industry button to pin on him and they have ropes to tie him with iffen he don't come easy.

30

'B illy!' I was at the window before I knew it, pushing Missus Kenny aside and sticking my head out as far as I could. 'Billy! Get offa the square, quick! The House of Industry men are coming to get you!'

Whether my waving caught folks' eyes or my yelling caught their ears, it seemed like the whole market stopped still. Faces turned up to the Misses Davies' windows, even some horses turned their heads. In the middle of it all Billy stared up at me, his familiar dark eyes huge, his hands already groping for his batons.

I had flung one hand towards the lane the men would come through. The folk in the market turned their heads, following my pointing finger towards the north end and then the whole fair sprang into action.

Two men grabbed Billy under the arms, swept him clean outta his bowl, and set off at a run towards the river end of the square. Another two grabbed his bowl and lifted it above their heads, running straight towards the distillery. A lad led the string of white ponies across the pathway, blocking it at one end, and another led a huge dray, cart an' all, across t'other. Someone else began to shovel manure into the middle of it, so that pathway all but disappeared in seconds. The older men took up the reins and ropes of their horses from the young boys. They began to lead their animals about, chuckling and nodding to each other. By the time the six House of Industry men entered the square, distinctive in their blue uniforms, the whole place had become a mass of moving men and horses, weaving and criss-crossing. From above it looked like the whole market was dancing some sort of clumsy dance. The musicians at the distillery gates began to play a hornpipe and the clack-clack of the horses' shoes on the cobbles near kept time.

The House of Industry men came to a startled halt. They tried to turn left; three huge plough horses were marking a ponderous circle. They tried to go straight ahead; a line of small ponies was running an ever-widening figure of eight. They made to turn back; an angry donkey was bucking and bellowing, kicking his back legs out furiously at all and sundry. The men plunged into the square, separating and squeezing off in any direction that would let them escape the flying hooves.

'Look at all that commotion!' Missus Kenny clutched my arm, screwing up her eyes and leaning out the window beside me. 'Where's poor Billy? Is he gettin' away?'

'I've lost sight of him, Missus Kenny,' I said, anxiously scanning the square, terrified that my early hesitation would cost Billy his freedom.

'There!' Miss Ruth cried, pointing at the south east end of the market. Miss Evelyn pushed her sister's arm down quickly but the House of Industry men were too mired in horseflesh to notice us up above their heads. One had just tripped over a wayward foot and was sprawled in dung below us. Another of them was trapped in a triangle of farmers who were waving pitchforks about and whistling and chatting like they didn't know he was there. Two more of the men were being chased up the square by a young fella riding bareback on the moon horse. He was yelling, 'Whoa!' and 'The divil mend it; it won't stop!' but we could all see he was in full control of the horse and enjoying the excuse to gallop clear through the centre of the market. Meanwhile we spotted the men what had Billy's bowl vanish into Jameson's Distillery.

'Ha!' Missus Kenny slapped her hand on the window ledge. 'Hide like with like.'

'What do you mean, Missus Kenny?' asked Miss Evelyn.

'I dare say they'll be after hidin' Billy's bowl amongst the half-made kegs in the cooper's yard,' Missus Kenny replied, chortling at the thought. 'The Industry men'll ne'er find it there unless they turn the whole place upside down an' they'll not be let do that. Ha!'

'I don't quite understand,' Miss Evelyn said. 'Surely they'd never take the boy's bowl?'

'Iffen they can't catch Billy today, then his bowl'll be the next best thing.' Missus Kenny scowled. 'Without it, they'll have him within the week.'

'Oh no!' Miss Ruth pointed again. 'They're catching up.'

The remaining two House of Industry men were big an' burly. They were pushing folk outta their way and they'd managed to get halfway down the square, heading in the right direction. Missus Kenny's hand tightened on my arm. The

Misses Davies' clutched each other. I could see Billy, still hanging between the two farmers, just ahead of his pursuers, only half a dozen folk separating them now.

Don't let them catch him, please don't let them catch him, I prayed.

Above all the noise came a shrill wolf whistle. Near the pursuers we saw a hand go up, furiously waving a red neckerchief and the boy on the moon horse came charging through the crowd in response. How everyone got outta his way, I don't know, but they did. He ran the horse in front of the two men, then turned sharply to cross their path again. This time he brought the horse to a stop and it reared high, giving them men no choice but retreat. Billy and his rescuers reached the corner of the square and turned down New Church Street, disappearing from sight.

Thank God, I thought. No matter what he'd done with my running-away money, I couldn't bear to think of him locked in that place.

As if by some signal, the whole market began to move. Every man and woman on it turned towards the centre, pulling their animals behind them. It only took a moment and the whole square came to a standstill. The two biggest House of Industry men were trapped like their friends, pushed and manhandled inwards. The circle tightened around them, an impenetrable wall of man and horse.

It was then the musicians took it into their heads to play a death march and the crowd became eerily quiet. The good-humoured camaraderie what had rescued Billy faded into cold anger at these men and the hated place they came from.

Everyone seemed to become still as stone, shoulders hunched, faces everywhere set into belligerent sneers. I watched the alarm of the trapped men turn to naked fear.

'Missus Kenny!' Miss Evelyn squeaked. 'They'll not – the crowd won't – they won't hurt those men?'

Her question hung in the air. Missus Kenny didn't answer; she drew her hand to her mouth like she was afraid to speak what was in her mind. The musicians stopped their death march, aware their joke had gone awry. The crowd pressed in closer. Miss Ruth hid her face in her hands and Miss Evelyn turned away. I didn't dare breathe.

'Easy, lads. Easy now!' A voice broke the silence below us and a figure, taller than any other, came pushing through the throng and stepped into that wee circle where the six men were standing huddled back to back. He said something to the men we couldn't hear then turned to the crowd.

'Job well done, my friends! Young Billy is safe.' Da's voice boomed across the square. 'We can all relax now, let these men go back where they come from. Sure aren't they just doin' their day's work like the rest o' us?'

'No dey-cent man would do it!' someone shouted.

'Don't we all have ta put potatoes in the pot, James Gibney?' asked Da, his voice calm but clear.

'You lost yer employment a while back, Milo Tyrell. Iffen a position comes free at the House o' Industry, will ye be takin' it?'

Da shrugged. 'Sure don't I have my good lady wife and me daughter out earnin'? Maybe I fancy bein' a man o' leisure for a while, just like the toffs on Sackville Street, don't ya know!' He whipped an old hankie from his pocket and struck a pose, one hand on his hip and the other waggling that hankie about like a dandy.

The crowd laughed.

'Now what'd'ya say we get this fair goin' again?' Da said. 'Are yez here to sell horses, or what?'

More laughter and people began to move away, leading their animals off to reclaim their usual places. Da looked at the House of Industry men and jerked his head towards Red Cow Lane. They didn't need telling twice. He walked with them all the way to the north of the square but no one was paying them any heed now. Those men would never go after Billy again.

Thanks be, I thought, one hand on my mouth, t'other on my belly. I took a couple of deep breaths. Billy was free. No one'd been hurt. Thanks be.

Up at our window Missus Kenny and the Misses Davies were happily moving away to their seats but I called them back. At the river end of the square the farmers had re-entered with Billy aloft on their shoulders. The crowd broke into a huge cheer. His bowl was fetched outta Jameson's just as quick. As Billy was placed back in it, he glanced up at our windows.

He waved. I hesitated then waved back.

His tentative smile became a grin, and he disappeared in a circle of well-wishers.

'Well done, Taney,' Miss Evelyn said. 'You and your dear father are heroes! Your premonition has saved Billy from that awful place. As for your papa – well!'

Missus Kenny nodded. 'Those men were lucky he came when he did, or they'd ha' been done for.' She wagged her finger at Horace who was sitting plum in the middle of the table, cleaning milk offa his whiskers.

There was no more talk of the Stoneybatter Strangler now, nor of the party at Number Eleven; the chat was all about Billy's great escape and Da's bravery. But I was drawn back to the window. I shuddered with a fresh jolt of shock as I remembered again what I'd seen that night on Grange Gorman Lane. The girl's staring eyes, her bonnet rolling.

He's out there, I thought. The strangler's out there, right now, down below me in the square. The feeling came over me fierce strong and for a horrible moment I had a notion that the strangler really might be someone I'd met, someone I knew. My skin crawled at the thought.

I scanned the crowd. Matt Davern was there, looking over a basket of squirming pups. There was the Hon John, the gentleman thief who had tried to steal Mistress Lacey's necklace. He was haggling over a bay tethered to a tree down the south end. From the corner of my eye, I saw Ed Manning stride onto the square from King Street. He still rented the attic room next to ours at the lodging house, though he wasn't a student no more. The penniless poet, Missus Kenny called him, but I could see he had a fine new cane today and he was wearing a decent pair of boots.

And, straight ahead of me, on t'other side of the square, standing outside the distillery gates, was Da. I was so proud of what he'd just done and yet I couldn't help thinking of how strange he'd become lately. From where I stood in the window his eyes were shaded by the brim of his old round hat, but I knew, certain-sure, they were staring right up at me.

31

Billy was waiting in the alley that evening when me and Mary Kate came home from charring.

'Mind yer back for yer supper, Taney, d'you hear?' was all Mary Kate said before she went upstairs.

I waited till we were at our old haunt by the stream before I rounded on him and all the anger and hurt came welling up from where I'd stuffed it down.

'How could you do it, Billy? How could you take the money what I gave you an' me thinking you were in trouble? An' then you just went an' played it all away. You're a liar and a thief, Billy Bowl.' I felt the tears start in my eyes but I blinked hard. I walked up and down the bank of the stream.

'I *was* in trouble, Taney, I swear I was. I wasn't lyin' about that.' Billy was stammering trying to get the words out quick. 'I owed that money to the Ormond Boys, just like I said, an' I meant to go straight an' give it them b-b-but then I got a better idea.'

I stopped pacing and glared at him. He couldn't look me in the eye. His hands were shaking like last time. He didn't bother trying to disguise it.

'I-I-I got to thinking how if I only had twice what you gave me I'd be able to pay off all a' what I owed, an' have a little left over. Then I thought o' that game they sometimes play behind The Half Moon of a Sunday afternoon.' He shrugged, only instead of his shoulders coming up to meet his ears, all nonchalant-like, his head sank downwards and he sat slouched in his bowl.

'And you lost it all?'

He nodded miserably. 'The Ormond Boys gave me a right hidin' a few days later.'

'You don't still owe them?'

He shook his head. 'I'd be dead iffen I did. An' maybe it'd be better iffen I was, an' all.' He attempted a laugh but it came out like a sob. It was then I noticed his eyes were too bright, like someone starting a fever, and they were flicking like moths what can't decide which flower to land on.

'You all right, Billy?' I asked, still a bit of sharpness in my voice, not ready to show I'd forgive him yet.

He looked down at the ground and shook his head. To my dismay, he began to cry. I couldn't bear it no more. I went to him, knelt in front of his bowl, and took his hand. He snatched it away. As he did I caught the stink of drink on his breath.

Jay, I thought. What's happened to him? It's like one of his black moods has swallowed him whole.

''Twas one o' the nuns sent the House o' Industry men after me.' He began to rock back and forth like that day in January by the river. 'Me old friend, Sister Brigid, met me on the street. She asked iffen I still say me prayers an' I told her I prayed that I'd win every time I laid a wager, an' I thanked

God every time I held a whiskey. She wagged her finger an' said me immortal soul was in danger an' I need to be saved from meself, and that 'twas in the House of Industry I belonged.' He attempted another laugh. 'Thing is, Taney, I do need savin' an' all. I can't think o' nothin' but the next game an' the next drink.'

He held his hands out in front of him and they quivering like leaves in autumn.

'See that?' he said. 'When I'm neither gamin' nor drinkin' me hands are shakin' fit ta fall offa me. I need yer help, Taney. I know as I've no right to ask after what I done but—'

He stopped. Something in my face musta made him unsure. His eyes were pleading with me.

I had the power to hurt him now.

For a moment I thought of walking away but I couldn't. I wanted his friendship back, even though a part of me would never forget what he'd done.

'I'll not go gaming again with you, Billy,' I said, frowning.

'I'll not ask you to,' he said real quick. 'Even iffen I wanted to, the story is out about you havin' second sight like yer mam. No one'd have you near a game again. No, that's not it at all. I need ta stop gamin'. It's destroyin' me, Taney.' His voice shook and his breath was coming hard and short.

'So stop going,' I said, but softly now.

'"Tis not that easy,' he said. 'Every day I swear I'll not go. An' every night I think, just one more game, one more wager.'

'You're going gaming *every* night?' I blinked.

He nodded. 'I was hopin' you'd be willin' to come meet

me of an evenin' ta keep me company, stop me goin', keep me outta mischief, like.'

'Meet you here, by the stream, like this?'

He nodded, and I could see the desperation in his eyes. He really meant what he said. At that moment, he meant it. 'Please, Taney. For old time's sake? I–I don't think I can do it without your help.'

I nodded slowly. It'd be like last summer, them early days when all we did was talk and laugh together. Just me and Billy. 'An' maybe you can keep me outta trouble an' all,' I said.

'What d'ya mean?'

'I been floating again and seeing things I don't want to see.'

Billy turned white. 'You never saw what happened t'other night?'

I nodded. My turn to shake now.

'But you didn't see his face, the strangler's?'

I shook my head. 'I'm scared stiff, Billy. I'm afraid it's someone I know.'

'Someone you know? Why would you think that?' He folded his arms, leaned back in his bowl and stared at me in horror.

'It feels close to me somehow. I–I can't explain. I've tried to tell myself 'tis nowt to do with me but something inside my head keeps tellin' me it is. Why else am I seeing it? Of all the bad things that happen in this city why am I pulled outta myself to see what he does?'

'But who could it be?' Billy spread his hands out, questioning.

'I don't know.'

'Well, then.' Billy shrugged.

'I'm afraid it's . . .' but my mouth went dry and I couldn't say it.

'Who? Who?' Billy's eyes were near popping out of his head.

'Me da,' I whispered.

For a moment Billy seemed stunned into silence. He sat back in his bowl and regarded me with his mouth open. Then he spluttered, 'Yer da? Yer *da*? Miles-high Tyrell? The man that stopped murder bein' done today in the market? Are you gone daft? You need ta stop that floatin'; 'tis turnin' yer brains ta porridge.'

The two of us began to laugh then. We laughed just like we used to. And when it was time to head home we agreed we'd meet every evening. I'd keep Billy from his gambling and drinking, and he'd keep me from floating, and we'd talk and laugh, just like we done the summer before.

32

That's how it was, for a short while. Billy'd collect me in the alley after supper and we'd make our way to the stream. When we were there, everything was grand. Billy was trying hard to make it up to me and I tried to distract him from his troubles with stories about the party to be held at Number Eleven. He told me stuff 'bout the nights he went gaming without me that'd make yer hair stand on end. Then Billy'd escort me back to Thundercut; Mary Kate and Da had made it a condition of me meeting Billy, on account of the strangler. They were good days; I was happy.

After about a week, though, Billy was shaking something awful and he'd begun to get right snappy. One minute he was arguing with everything I said, next he wasn't even listening.

'Let's go fly down Kiss-arse-lane!' I suggested once, trying to humour him.

''Tis too far.'

'It's only over the river,' I said. 'Come on, Billy. We'll be there in no time. It'll be fun.' I jumped to my feet but Billy shook his head and stared at his hands.

'I'm too tired ta roll all that way just ta fling meself down a bloomin' hill,' he said.

'Ah, come on, Billy,' I insisted, nudging his shoulder to encourage him.

'No, I said!' He shook me away roughly. 'Leave off! Let me be.'

I put my fists on my hips and glared at him. 'Who asked who to be here for them every evening?' I demanded.

He glowered back at me a moment then dropped his eyes. I sat down crossly and wondered why I bothered. I watched the brook bubble by, my mind wandering to Miss Clary and the party at Number Eleven, where all would be bright and dainty.

After a while Billy said how he was sorry, and it was hard for him 'cause he wanted to go gaming so bad it was all he could think about. An' I said it was all right, I didn't mind, and we could race down Keyser's Lane another evening.

But I knew we wouldn't. Billy had changed. So had I, for that matter. I was beginning to understand that iffen I wanted a better life for myself just dreaming wouldn't get me it. I'd have to reach out and take it.

Next night he was snarling and nasty and rude again.

'Miss Clary says this an' Miss Clary does that,' he snapped. 'Iffen she tolt you to stand on yer head, you would! Be the plain folk o' Dublin not good enough for you no more, Taney Tyrell? Plannin' on risin' above us all, is that it? Yer a ninny with yer dreams o'runnin' away to London an' becomin' a favourite o' the toffs. Ye'll come a cropper an' end up on the streets, more like!'

I was so shocked that for a moment I couldn't speak. Tears

smarted in my eyes to hear my dreams made silly and small. By Billy.

'Take that back!' I gasped.

'Not iffen it's true!' He shrugged and turned his back to me.

'Go stuff yourself, Billy Bowl,' I yelled, and I stomped off home on my own.

Next day he was in the alley, all sweetness again. He begged my forgiveness and made me promise I'd be there every night, even iffen he'd been in a black mood day before, for that was when he needed me most, he said.

Billy needed me. So long as he did, I'd be there for him. He was my best friend and I loved him, d'you see. I was determined to help him however hard he made it. Though I'd not let him use me like before; I'd never let anyone do that again.

Over the next few evenings he got quieter and quieter. Then there was an evening he hardly said a word, just sat in his bowl, sunk down, messing with something in his right hand.

'What'ya got there, Billy?' I asked, when I couldn't bear the silence no longer.

He uncurled his fingers. In his palm lay a single white dice.

The next evening Billy didn't came calling. I waited in Thundercut Alley a whole hour but he never came.

33

I t was the evening of the party at Number Eleven. Mary Kate had been working all day at the house helping to get things ready, but Mistress Lacey said I was to stay home and rest so as to be fresh for the night ahead. To my surprise, when it was time to go, Da followed me to the backstairs.

'I'll not have ya walkin' the streets alone,' was all he said.

'What about Jon Jon?' I said, looking over to where my wee brother was already dozing on the big mattress. 'I'll be all right. It's still bright out.'

''Twill only take minutes ta walk you that far. Jon Jon's asleep; he won't know I'm gone.' Da grabbed his hat.

When we came out into the alley I looked about me in case Billy had come, but he hadn't. Me and Da walked up towards Queen Street in silence. I began thinking about the fancy costume I was to wear to play the part of the gypsy fortune teller, but as we left the alley something made me glance back.

Billy was there. In the shadows at the bend.

Da turned to see what was holding me up. When he saw Billy watching us from the depths of the alley, he shook his head.

'You'll not be meetin' him tonight,' he said to me. 'You've

taken on a job o' work at the Laceys'. I don't approve o' it but you've said you'll do it so you'll not be lettin' them down now.'

He cupped his hands to his mouth. 'Taney's workin' tonight, Billy,' he hollered.

I thought I saw Billy nod and begin to turn his bowl but it was hard to be sure in the twilight. Da put his hand on my shoulder and walked me away. He left me at the railings of Number Eleven without another word said 'tween us.

I paused at the top of the basement steps and looked back towards the alley. Billy hadn't come calling last three nights, and I'd waited for him every one.

Maybe he's in trouble, I thought, frustrated that he'd turned up again the one night I couldn't meet him. What's he been doing the last few nights? What if he owes the Ormond Boys money again?

I'll find him tomorrow, I promised myself, and iffen it's money he needs, I'll give him some o' what I earn tonight. Not all of it, mind, not this time. And I'll go with him to pay them butcher boys, make sure he does it.

Satisfied that I'd do my best by Billy soon as I could, I ran down the steps into the mayhem of Missus Mangan's kitchen, where an extra cook and several servants had been hired in for the night.

'Yer to go straight up to Miss Hickson's room,' Missus Mangan barked, without even turning her head from the stove.

Mary Kate looked up from the table where she was setting trays. She pursed her lips and gave a curt nod. ''Cepta was in the scullery cleaning oysters, crying over how they were cutting her fingers. Rob was busy fetching and carrying, wheezing as usual. One of the pimples on his neck had grown into an angry boil. He passed me a bit of gingerbread from the table while Missus Mangan wasn't looking, and I grabbed it and scarpered.

On the way upstairs I peeped in the parlour door. Two musicians were practising in a corner and Mistress Lacey was directing men to hang ribbons and light lanterns.

In the attic Miss Clary and Miss Hickson were already in costume. In all the excitement now I let my worries 'bout Billy slip to the back of my mind. Miss Clary was dressed as a shepherdess and her governess was a milkmaid. Not that I'd ever seen a shepherdess nor a milkmaid dressed in silk with fine lace at their wrists and on their aprons, and shiny satin shoes with silver buckles on their white stockinged feet! My lovely gypsy gown and all the jewellery I was to wear lay on Miss Hickson's bed.

'Come in, Taney, and we'll get you ready,' Miss Clary announced loudly into the corridor, then pulled me into the room and closed the door.

'Tonight is the night, Taney!' she said, and winked.

'You mean the party?' But I knew she didn't. 'You mean ...?' I looked from her to Miss Hickson who suddenly seemed confused, excited and scared all at once.

'She's going to do it; she's going to *elope!*' Miss Clary whispered this last word into my ear, though none could hear but we three. 'She will feign a headache early in the evening and excuse herself from the party, then steal away to meet

Uncle Richard.' She smiled and her blue eyes twinkled. 'My Uncle Richard is a darling, Taney, and so very handsome!'

I smiled at Miss Hickson. 'Everything will be all right now,' I said. "Tis the only way.'

Miss Hickson nodded. 'There is one thing I should like to be sure of, Taney. If – when I do this, when I—'

'*Elope!*' Miss Clary whispered.

'I will see Clary again, won't I?' Miss Hickson reached for Miss Clary's hand. 'Mistress Lacey will forgive her brother? She will forgive me? She wouldn't be so unkind as to keep Clarissa and myself apart?'

I turned away to finger the finery waiting for me on the bed. 'You and Miss Clary will meet again. 'Course you will,' I said as firmly as I could. And 'twere true enough. They would meet again, but only when Mistress Lacey was in her grave, and Miss Clary was a married woman, free of her mother's influence.

'There, you see? I told you how it would be.' Miss Clary clapped her hands. 'Now, Taney, we must make a gypsy of you and get you downstairs before our esteemed guests arrive!'

34

'But I *will* marry?' The girl sitting across the table from me was becoming petulant. And probably near as hot as me, though she had a fan that she was swishing impatiently. I leaned in and tried to catch some of its beats.

My gypsy tent was very pretty indeed and had drawn much admiration from the ladies as they'd entered the front parlour. I had also been much commented on, my bonny green jacket, the gay coloured gown, my hair caught back in the striped gypsy scarf, my earrings and bangles; but truth is that after a while the scarf was slipping over my eyes every other minute and the gown itched. The day had been the first truly nice one of the year and the parlours were rather warm despite the open windows and doors. The tent became like an oven inside, what with its lantern hung above my head so as to make me look mysterious, and the door flap closed over to give each fortune-seeker privacy. I had been in here for at least two hours now and had only read leaves for half the room.

I wondered iffen Miss Hickson had slipped away to meet her sweetheart as planned. I wondered where Billy was. Getting himself into more trouble? Probably. Well, I would just have to help pick up the pieces tomorrow, wouldn't I?

Once Billy'd been my rescuer; now it was me saving him.

'Well?' The girl rapped her fan on the table to get my attention.

I peered in her cup. 'I see a vase, which means you have a secret admirer, miss, but it's too soon to tell iffen – I mean if – you'll marry him.' I decided not to mention that I could decipher a mouse in the leaves – thief of hearts. I yawned.

'Well, if my future is boring you I shall most certainly bother you no longer,' she said loudly, pushing back her chair so hard it fell over and near took my little tent with it.

She flounced out into the room and let the tent flap close behind her. I sank down on the table. My head was spinning from too many questions, too many futures, too many voices. Outside the tent food was being served and card tables had been set up to keep everyone amused while they waited their turn with the gypsy girl. Missus Mangan, with a face on her what'd curdle milk, was standing by the table making fresh pots of tea each time they ran out.

I'd read for twelve of the women so far. When will I marry? Will he be handsome? Will he be rich? How many children will I have? Will I live to be old? Everyone, the same questions, and each one wanting so much from me that Mistress Lacey had to politely suggest a time limit be put on how long they each could have with me. My head was splitting and, to make things worse, the musicians were playing a fast reel. All twenty-five women were talking at once it seemed. Every now and then someone would shriek or squeal at some new bit of gossip and it would shoot through my head like an arrow. I closed my eyes and tried to make my mind quiet.

Suddenly I was outside, suspended above the street. He was there, the strangler. I could sense him in the shadows, staring straight at the house. The basement door opened below me. Someone came out, a woman. She set a valise on the ground and closed the door quietly behind her. She began to ascend the steps, holding her grey petticoat up in one hand and clutching her bag in the other. At the top she looked up and down anxiously.

Alone on the street.

Where he was.

I started awake.

'What did you say to Lady Ann? She has taken it sorely amiss.' Mistress Lacey's voice all of a sudden hissed in my ear. She glared at me through the tent flap.

I jumped to my feet. 'I'm sorry, ma'am. It's just so hot in here, ma'am,' I mumbled, trying to step around her, pushing her outta my way in my distress. 'Where's Miss Clary? I need to find Miss Clary.'

I ignored Mistress Lacey's furious glare and stumbled out into the parlour. 'Miss Clary!' I shouted over the din. 'Miss Clary, where's Miss Hickson?'

35

'Miss Hickson retired to her room with a headache a half an hour ago, girl!' Mistress Lacey stepped in front of me and grabbed my wrist. She spoke low through clenched teeth then flashed a smile around the room. 'Her whereabouts are of no matter. You are here to entertain our guests: do it!' she said, pushing me back towards the little tent.

Miss Clary appeared behind her mother. 'Can't you see she needs a rest, Mama? Come, Taney, have some cake and a small glass of wine.' She frowned at her mother and led me over to an open window where I gratefully took a few deep breaths.

'Miss Hickson has gone,' she whispered. 'Ten minutes or more ago. What's wrong?'

'You're sure it was as long as ten minutes ago?' I faltered. I'd have sworn I'd been floating but the timing was wrong. And iffen it had been a premonition I should have seen it before it happened, not after.

Miss Clary nodded. 'I watched her go from the dining room window. Uncle Richard was to meet her just outside on the street but at the last moment he sent a message to meet him on Prussia Street. He was worried about Mama spotting his carriage.'

'You saw her walk away? You watched her as far as the corner?'

She shook her head, alarm in her eyes now. 'Mama called me. I didn't want her to come to the window so I had to move away.'

I stared down onto the street; it was empty. I shut my eyes and concentrated but I could see nothing else, I could feel nothing else. The sense of danger was passing. Perhaps I had imagined it. I didn't often confuse dreams with visions but tonight my head was a whirl with too many voices.

Miss Clary was trying to hide her concern. 'Do you think Miss Hickson is in danger?'

'I–I must be mistaken,' I stuttered. Maybe I was.

'Have some wine.' Miss Clary pressed a glass into my fingers.

I smiled weakly and took a sip. 'Don't them musicians know no slow airs?' I asked, pushing the scarf back outta my eyes again.

Miss Clary laughed. 'I'll go and inquire of them, directly.'

I stared out the window into the street. Was Miss Hickson all right? I shivered. Had the strangler been out there, watching this house, watching her? Had I imagined it all? I couldn't sense him now. Iffen he had been there he was gone.

I could see the darkness of Thundercut Alley skulking

between the houses on t'other side of the street. That 'minded me of Billy again. He was in trouble, I was sure of it. And here was me telling silly fortunes to silly girls and drinking wine.

Where are you, Billy? I thought. What are you doing?

I mopped my forehead with my birthday hankie, pulled the scarf back into place and tried to eat some cake.

'Apparently the poor girl was strangled practically outside her own home!' someone was saying behind me.

'There've been other incidents roundabout,' someone else replied. 'All of them servant girls.'

'All robbed of their wages,' the eldest Miss Wilkie trilled from the sofa.

'And all of them murdered?'

'No, only that one girl. The other victims survived but could give no clear description to the police.'

'I heard there've been four attacks altogether.'

'Five.'

'I heard six.'

Miss Wilkie caught sight of me at the window. 'But we can ask our fortune teller!' In the background the musicians slowed their bows and Miss Wilkie's strident voice drew the attention of the whole room. 'Gypsy Girl! Tell us true, what is the identity of the Stoneybatter Strangler?'

All the eyes of the room turned to me, all the faces looming white in the candlelight. Miss Wilkie's voice seemed to stretch and bend around my head, echoing weirdly.

The women's faces blurred and swam. The noise of their thoughts invaded mine, followed by the familiar nausea, the intense silence. I felt my spirit slide away to the window. I heard my body thump to the floor as I floated away into the darkness.

36

There's a little boreen offa Arbour Hill, behind the main barracks. It's called Richardson's Lane. That's where I fly, quick/fast. That's where he'll be. The strangler. I just know it.

It's long gone ten o'clock but it being May/time, there are people still abroad on the green and on the hill, courtin' couples out walking and cuddling. Oxmantown Green is dotted with lanterns but Arbour Hill is dark and Richardson's Lane is darker still. I peer about. There's a rubbish heap looming behind a wall part/way down the lane. I float closer. He's there. I can't see him but I can sense him. He's hiding, tensed like a spider, waiting to see who wanders into his web.

Closer.

I can hear him breathing heavily. I can smell the sour stale smell of the rubbish heap. It reminds me of something, but I can't recall what.

I retreat to the junction with Arbour Hill. Some people are walking there. Most will pass the lane and walk on down Montpelier Hill, but one of them will turn up this lonely wee road. Off in the distance I see a woman approaching from Prussia Street.

A tall slender young woman.

Yellow-haired.

In a grey travelling gown.

Carrying a valise.

No! No! It can't be Miss Hickson, it can't be, I tell myself.

But, whoever she is, she's going to walk straight into the strangler's arms. I can feel panic flood through me. It's happening again. He's going to kill again.

I'm torn between floating up the street to look at the woman, to see her face, and going back towards the rubbish heap to see his. I do neither, just hover, terrified. She's coming closer. He's heard her footfalls. I hear him clear his throat softly, ready to call out for help when she comes near.

Do something, ninny! I scream at myself. Go closer. Go see who he is.

But I can't. I'm too afraid of what I'll see. For I've suddenly thought what that sour smell 'minds me of. It's a smell I've caught often of late. It's the smell I've caught offa my da.

37

'A re you all right, Taney? Say something, please.' Miss Clary was leaning over me on the floor and at least a dozen more faces were staring down at me, all big-eyed and curious.

'Take another sip of wine,' she said. 'Don't sit up too quickly.'

I pushed the glass away. My mind is reeling with horror. Da! It must have been him outside on the street watching this house, watching Miss Hickson come up from the basement.

'What colour gown was Miss Hickson wearing when she left?' I whispered in Miss Clary's ear, hoping against hope that what I saw earlier was wrong.

'Grey.' I felt my face blanch and Miss Clary's eyes flared wide. She dropped the wine glass. It hit the rug and the red liquid splashed all that encircling white muslin. The women squealed and stepped back.

'I have to go,' I said. I struggled to my feet, pushed through the sea of petticoats, and lurched towards the door. Miss Clary tried to hold me but I shook myself free.

'The strangler's going to attack again; I have to stop him!' I kept my voice low as I could but them that was nearest heard me, and gasped. I ignored them. I ignored all the exclamations and questions and grasping hands; I had to get outta that house. I only stopped to grab one of the lanterns and then fled down the stairs and through the front door, as it was nearest.

Once on the street I made for Arbour Hill the shortest way – over the green. I ran a line straight through it till I reached the road on t'other side. I turned left, between the back of the barracks and its hay yard, towards Richardson's Lane. I ran a stitch into my side but I knew no matter how fast I went it were too late. By now the deed was done. He'd a' made his play of being hurt and needing help. The woman in the grey gown – Miss Hickson, oh God, it's Miss Hickson – had gone to his aid and he'd a' closed his hands around her neck.

Please don't kill her, I thought. Please let me get there to stop you this time. Please, Da, please.

I just reached the mouth of the lane when the night was pierced by a long shrill scream.

I stopped, frozen with fear.

'Help! Help! Help!' The words came shrieking from the shadows. Someone was groaning. Someone else was sobbing. 'Help us! Fer pity's sakes, someone help us!'

From behind me, the clatter of heavy boots on the road. Two night watchmen pushed past me and disappeared into the lane. I didn't follow; I knew nothing I did now would change anything. I could only stand at the mouth of the lane and wait. There was a roar and some scuffling. Raised angry voices.

'The bloody brute!' A woman's voice, shouting. 'He had

her be the neck! I only got here in nick o' time!'

'I've got him!' One of the watchmen, I guessed.

'Pin him down, don't let him get away!' The other one.

'Ohh, ohh, ohh!' A young woman's voice, sobbing.

She was alive, alive. Miss Hickson was alive. Thanks be for that.

'Are you all right? Can ya stand up, pet?' The first woman again.

'Ohh, ohh!' came the reply.

'I can't see a bloomin' thing,' and 'I've got him, I tell ya!' The watchmen.

'Stabbed him with me hatpin, I did. The brute! That'll learn him.' The first woman, indignantly.

'Wait a minute, this can't be right! Here, Joseph, give us a hand. Pull him into the light so as we can see what we've got.'

My relief that Miss Hickson was safe and no one had been murdered this night only lasted a single moment. Now came the sound of footsteps, petticoats swishing, and something heavy being dragged towards me. I stepped backwards, I could barely breathe. My heart seemed to have leapt into my throat and my knees were threatening to buckle.

Da, Da, Da, I thought.

A sorry little group emerged from the darkness of Richardson's Lane onto Arbour Hill. I swallowed hard and held up my lantern, steadying myself to look on the face of the Stoneybatter Strangler.

There was a sobbing young woman being helped by a large woman whose hat had come askew. The younger woman was wearing a grey gown but I saw at once she was not Miss Hickson.

A sob shuddered through my body. I was wrong about her. Please let me be wrong about Da too. Please let me be all wrong.

There were the two watchmen, flushed and scuffed, proudly hauling their prisoner between them.

There was the strangler, on the ground, one hand pressed against his left eye and the other dragging in the dirt. He seemed only half-conscious but he recognised me when he looked up, blinking one eye in the light of my lantern.

'Taney,' he mumbled. 'Why didn't you meet me like you promised? Why did you leave me alone tonight when I came fer ye?'

38

I fell down onto my knees and took Billy's face in my hands.
I couldn't speak. My mouth worked but nowt came out.

'Careful, miss,' one of the watchmen said. 'He's terrible
dangerous, he is.'

Billy, I thought.

'He's a monster!' the large woman exclaimed. 'He'd a'
killed our Kitty iffen I hadn't got there. Monster!'

I shook my head. Billy. It can't be. Billy.

'We've reason to suspect he's a murderer, miss, an' that he
killed that wee girl up Grange Gorman Lane.'

'No, no. He didn't mean to,' I tried to say, but the words
came out all shaken and mangled. I could only stare at Billy
in disbelief. There was blood running down his face from
where the woman had stabbed him with her pin. He was
shaking his head at me, one hand still pressed to the injured
eye.

'I didn't mean it, Taney,' he whispered. 'I never meant for
that – I only wanted her money, was all. You know that, don't
ya, Taney? You know I never meant—'

'Wha's that he's sayin'? Is it confessin' he is?' The older

watchman pushed me aside. 'You'll be a witness to it. Wha'd he say?'

'I don't know.' I shrugged desperately. 'I don't know what he said.'

'Come away, Taney dear.' Someone took my hand and tugged me back a little. 'Twas then I became aware that Miss Clary had followed me from the house, and a half a dozen or more of the toff girls, an' all. They were standing huddled behind her, looks of horrified delight on their painted faces. Over their shoulders I could see more people approaching from the direction of Oxmantown Green, and other folk were coming up the hill.

'Is it true?' a young fella called to us. 'Have they caught the strangler?'

'It's true!' The youngest Miss Wilkie suddenly found her voice. 'And he's standing right here!'

'Well, he's not exactly standin', miss,' the younger watchman said. 'An' he couldn't iffen he tried, him havin' no legs to start with.'

'He has no legs?' This was fairly shrieked by the young ladies, and they stepped closer to see for themselves. 'He's got no legs, the strangler has no legs.'

The young fella had reached us by now. 'Jay!' he said, shocked. 'It's that Billy-the-bowl!' He turned back the road and cupped his hands to his mouth. 'Come see,' he roared. 'They've caught the strangler and it's Billy-the-bowl!'

Folk began to run forward till a small crowd was gathered.

'Is it daft yez are?' a man asked the watchmen. 'That's no strangler, 'tis just Billy-no-legs.'

It *is* daft, I thought. Billy can't have done them things. How could he have? But in my mind everything was crashing into place – things I'd seen, things I hadn't wanted to see.

The large woman stepped forward brandishing her hatpin. 'He may have no legs but he was quick enough to use them big hands o' his to throttle me poor cousin. He's stronger than you, I'd say, fer all him has but arms.'

The crowd considered this. All the while Billy kept his head down, his long hair hiding his face as he moaned quietly to himself and knuckled one eye. I crept forward again and took his other hand in mine.

'What's she doin' here?' A girl built near as wide as she was tall broke away from her lad and pointed at me. 'She's his friend, so she is, and she needn't deny it,' she announced loudly.

'I don't deny it,' I said, straightening up. 'I am his friend. I am Billy-the-bowl's friend.'

And I should have been there for him tonight, like I promised, I thought. Iffen I could just have the time again, iffen I could just have another chance . . .

'She's his friend, she says she's his friend,' rippled through the crowd.

This would never have happened, iffen I'd have kept my word. Billy, I'm sorry. Forgive me.

'Taney,' Miss Clary whispered, and tugged on my arm again. 'Come away, Taney.'

'She's not just his friend, I'd say.' The girl spoke up for all to hear. 'I'd say she's his accomplice. Sure an' he'd never have managed to do what he done by his self.'

'But she wasn't there,' the hatpin woman protested. 'She wasn't in the lane.'

'She was right here when we came out o' it, though,' said the younger watchman.

'*And* she was here when we went in,' said the older. 'Why was she standin' here iffen she'd nowt ta do with it? What are you doin' here, miss?' he said, lifting his lantern and shining it into my face.

'I-I . . .' What could I say? Iffen I told them the truth they'd never believe me.

'She was with us all evening,' Miss Clary said. 'I can vouch for her.'

'An' who might you be, miss?'

'An' why are yez dressed so queer?' This from a man in the crowd. Miss Clary looked down at her fancy dress and I looked down at mine. We musta looked a sight, a 'gypsy' and a 'shepherdess', and behind us two more 'shepherdesses', three 'milkmaids' and two 'country lasses'. I pulled the scarf offa my head.

'She fancies herself a witch,' said the big girl. 'And they used say her mam was one, an' all.'

'I've seen you before, you with the red hair.' A man came forward, leaned down and stared right at me. 'An' you was with Billy Bowl.' He shoved me sharply with his finger. 'The Hazard game out back The Half Moon, it was.'

'Aye, I seen her there too.'

'She *is* with him.'

'She's in on it! Like yer wan says, he can't have done it all be his self.'

'There's a pair o' them in it, murderers both.'

'She's guilty as he is.'

'She's NOT!' Billy looked up suddenly from the ground. 'She's not with me. She's not me friend. She was never me friend. She's a fool, a little fool. I made use o' her for cheatin' at cards twice or thrice an' I used ta cadge money offa her when I needed it. She's nothin' but a stupid ninny.' He spat in my direction; it landed on my petticoat.

I stared at him and he looked back, his face all cold, like he'd meant what he'd just said.

He can't mean it, I thought.

But he's betrayed you before, a small hurt voice inside me said. And didn't you often think . . .

No! I shook my head. He's bluffing them, you ninny. Like at the Hazard games. Only he's trying to win you a way outta this mess.

I tried to smile, to show him that I understood, that I knew he was just saying those things so as they'd leave me alone.

The crowd were all mumbling now and I leaned down close as I could so hardly no one else could hear. 'Forgive me, Billy,' I whispered. 'I'm sorry I wasn't there tonight, like you asked.'

He scowled at me then lowered his head but under his black hair he looked at me with his uninjured eye. His mouth formed my name. 'Go, Taney,' he was saying. 'Get outta here.'

Through the growing grumbles of the crowd I half-heard, half-lip-read, 'Don't let them take you too, Taney. Get away,' and, 'Fer God's sake, Taney, don't let me have more blood on me hands.' Least, that's what I thought he said.

'He's talkin' to her, I'm tellin' yez,' the girl bellowed, and everyone was staring at me again.

I tried to grab his hand, to hold on to him, but Billy pushed me away. He snarled and sat up straight. Then he took his hand away from his left eye. The crowd groaned and leaned closer to see all the blood and mess where the hatpin had gone in. Eyes squeezed shut in horror then popped wide to look again. Mouths stretched and squirmed into grimaces made hideous by the jumping shadows thrown by the watchmen's lamps. I was forgot; everyone was squealing and pointing, jabbing the air around Billy with their accusing fingers, moving closer.

'Murderer,' they said.

'Monster.'

'Devil.'

'Billy,' I whispered, but someone was pulling me back and I couldn't see him no more; the crowd closed in about him. I heard him howl – long, sad, desperate, like a lost dog.

'Come away, Taney,' Miss Clary said again, urgently, picking my lantern up from where I'd abandoned it. I stumbled and protested but she had a firm hold of my arm and she tugged me along the street, the little gaggle of toffs in their fancy dress scurrying after us.

39

Miss Clary kept a grip of me and fair ran us all the way back to Queen Street. She looked over her shoulder several times to check iffen anyone had followed us, but no one had. The front door of Number Eleven was ajar when we reached it and most of the women we had left in the front parlour were outside on the top step, a bevy of moths fluttering under the door lamp.

'There you are!' they cried as we approached. 'Where have you been? You'll never guess what has happened here while you were gone!'

They all began to speak at once, their voices so many and so shrill that not one word could be understood. Not that I cared less at that moment for knowing what these silly women were yaddering about. I could think only of Billy. Billy – alone with that mob.

'Fer the love o' God, BE QUIET!' a harsh voice bawled above the lot of them. Missus Mangan stepped out from the hallway, through the front door.

'Has Mrs Mangan lost her mind?' Miss Clary asked me, under her breath.

I shrugged. All I wanted now was to go home but Miss Clary's hand had tightened on my wrist.

'What's happened, Mrs Mangan?' she demanded, her voice ringing clear though there was fear jumping into her eyes. 'Is it bad news of Miss Hickson? Where is my mother?'

'Miss Clarissa.' Missus Mangan rose to her full height. 'Yer mother is indisposed. She had to retire to her boo-dwar all o' a sudden an' she left her guests in my charge.' The housekeeper pursed her lips. 'An' I don't mind sayin' it, seen as 'tis not a word o' a lie, but they have abused Mistress Lacey's hospitality something shockin'.' She glared at the women on the steps. One or two of them looked down at their feet and more of them giggled right into Missus Mangan's face.

'Miss Lacey! Your dear mama has had the most shocking news!' one announced, her voice honeyed with concern but her mouth unable to stop itself forming a spiteful smile. 'It seems your governess, Miss Hickson, has run away in the night!'

'Eloped!' said another.

'With your uncle!' Lady Ann spluttered.

I felt Miss Clary's grip relax. 'Is that all?' she said.

'All?' Lady Ann looked down her small nose. 'Your uncle has married beneath him. Your looks, education and prospects are not ample enough to compensate for *such* connections.'

Thanks be that Miss Hickson has taken hold of happiness, I thought wearily. Thanks be some good has come of this awful night.

Miss Clary ignored Lady Ann and turned to Missus Mangan. 'Is there a note from Miss Hickson?' she asked, her voice a little sharp. 'Is that where this news has come from?'

The housekeeper became flustered. She opened her mouth several times like a fish.

''Tweren't me fault,' she began. 'I was only tryin' to do what I thought best. The note come when you was out. You'd left so sudden, running after *her*– she scowled at me, clearly of the opinion that I was the root of all this evil, – 'so I give it your mother. When she read it she had an attack o' the vapours an' the bloomin' thing musta slid outta her hand to the floor. While me an' Mary Kate helped Mistress Lacey up to her boo⁄dwar, one o' them *ladies* picked it up an' read it to all an' sundry, like it was a common broadside, not a private letter what is none o' *their* business to touch, let alone read!' She huffed and folded her arms.

''Tis so romantic!' 'Cepta chimed in, all of a sudden appearing outta the shadows.

Everyone looked at her in astonishment. She clasped both hands to her chest and her eyes were shiny with tears. 'Miss Hickson wrote as how she was in her beau's carriage an' he about ta sweep her away into the night.' She waved one arm across the sky in an arc, as if Miss Hickson and her lover were to ride clear over the moon. 'They're to be married be a vicar at midnight! Missus Mangan, ma'am, is it midnight yet? Is it done?'

40

Miss Clary let go my hand then and I slipped away. Thundercut Alley was dark as ever. When I turned down it I remembered the night, months back, when the strangler had been there, waiting for me.

The strangler.

Billy.

How could I not ha' seen it? I thought of the sweating and rocking and the grey colour of his face the day by the river. And how he said he needed savin' from his self after the House of Industry men tried to catch him.

And I'd not come. I'd not come to him when he'd said he needed my help. I'd dressed up in a silly costume and played parlour games with the Quality instead.

The tears started as I put my hand to the alley door. I wanted to bury my head in my blanket and hide from the world. But the door wouldn't open, having been locked at seven bells for fear of the strangler. I sank down to the ground in the dark, sat in the dirt and wailed.

That's how Mary Kate found me, when she came. She put her arms around me and held me till my sobbing died down enough to get me up the stairs. She sat me in me da's chair and put a cup of milk into my hands.

'Billy—'

'I know,' she said, stroking my hair. 'Miss Clary told me. She told me it all. She told me to come home to you, that you'd be needin' me.'

I nodded.

'Billy Bowl attacked those girls: he's the Stoneybatter Strangler.' She shook her head. 'Such charm an' such wickedness in one lad. I can't believe it.'

'Billy isn't wicked.' I pulled away from her.

'If he's what they say he is then he's done some terrible wicked things.'

I couldn't deny it so I tried to excuse it. 'He got into trouble gambling. And I think he was drinking too. He needed the money.'

'Does that make what he done all right?'

I shook my head. 'He never meant to kill that girl.'

She eyed me sharply. 'How d'you know that? Have you known it was him all along?'

'No, never. Not till tonight. I thought it was – it might be – I mean . . . I thought it was . . . me da.'

'Yer da?' Her eyes flew open wide and I think she almost laughed. 'Yer da? Whatever made you think that?'

'He was out every night there was an attack. And he's been acting queer, not like his self. And there's the smell: he's been smelling queer, an' all.'

She sighed. 'Yer da's been rubbish pickin' of a night to earn a few pennies to put towards our keep. It mortifies him something terrible not to be earnin' at all but he'd rather you think he was out drinkin' every night then doin' something so low. That's where he'll be now. Missus Kenny knows — she's mindin' Jon Jon since darkness fell — but you're not to let on. It'd kill him fer certain iffen he knew you knew.'

'You won't tell him what I thought?'

'That he might be the strangler? No, I'll not.'

'What'll they do to Billy? They'll not — they'll never h⁄ hang him?'

'That's what they do to murderers, Taney. He may not ha' meant to, but he took that girl's life all the same.'

I let out a wail. I think I'd have turned hysterical only Mary Kate grabbed me and gave me a shake.

'Hold yourself together, pet,' she said. 'There's no time for that now.'

I nodded and gulped. I pushed my horror back to where I could bear it: over in the corner, lurking where I could see it outta the side of my eye, not right inside me where it'd tear me all apart. I tried to see what the future held for Billy but I'd never been able to tell nothing 'bout him before, and I couldn't now neither. And yet ... hadn't I always sensed the strangler was someone close? Was it my friendship with Billy that had caused me to float to the scenes of the stranglings?

I looked back, trying to see what I'd missed and iffen I could have stopped things turning out this way. I remembered the night in Kiss⁄arse⁄lane when Billy had said there had to be more to life, even for the likes of us. But there wasn't much else for Billy than begging.

'We need to pack yer things.' Mary Kate stood up abruptly.

'What? Why?'

'Miss Clary told me what the crowd were sayin', Taney. They're makin' out you had somewhat to do with it all. Folk round here were that fond o' Billy they'll be very happy to blame someone else. An' if the police decide you may have been involved you could go to jail. Iffen they were to find you guilty o' murder . . .' She crossed herself. 'You can't stay here now. We've got to get you away, an' quick.'

41

My few belongings were already tied up in a cloth by the time Da came in. He saw the bundle in middle of floor, looked from it to me, and began to cry. I flew into his arms and he held me like he'd never let go.

'You heard what's happened?' Mary Kate said over my head.

He nodded.

'She can't stay.'

'I know,' he said. 'But what are we to send her away on? We've nowt.'

Mary Kate put her hand inside her petticoat and drew out fistfuls of coins. 'There's near eighteen shillin' all told. Miss Clary give it me. 'Tis what Taney earned tonight from readin' leaves. The Quality were beside themselves it seems. They'd never had a night like it afore, so they were generous.'

'Thank God for it,' Da said. 'That'll buy passage to England, Taney, and maybe put a roof over yer head for a while, iffen yer careful with it.'

I nodded. All the past year I'd been dreaming of running away but it had always been far in the future. Now it was here, I was afraid.

'You'll be all right,' Mary Kate said. 'You're young an' strong an' you've got a quick mind. You can char for a bit, an' when you've got the measure o' the folk about you, you can try your fortune tellin'. Only be careful, mind.'

I don't know which of us was more shocked by this unexpected pronouncement, me or Da.

'She's not goin' to give up usin' her gifts, Milo, that's become plain. I'm not sure that she could iffen she wanted to, but she's not like her mother so she'll be safe enough, I'm thinkin'.'

Da let me go, nodding to her as he turned away.

'What d'ya mean I'm not like my mother?' I asked, bristling. 'What does she mean, Da?'

'Milo?' Mary Kate put her hands on her hips and set her chin. 'She has a right ta know. I've always said 'twould be best to tell her. Milo?'

'I can't,' Da said.

'You must. I'll fetch Jon Jon,' Mary Kate said brusquely, and left the room.

Da began to pace. 'Yer mam,' he began. 'You have her looks an' gifts, yer so like her in some ways, but ...' He collapsed into his chair and drew his hands over his face. I sat on the floor beside him and waited.

'She was ... gentle. Too gentle for this world. It was one o' the things that drew me to her when we first met,' Da said. 'An' when I found out about her gifts an' how difficult she found it to cope with the things she saw, well, I just wanted ta protect her.'

'Did you love her?' I asked.

'Very much.' He stared over my head. 'She was so lovely. An' I could provide fer her an' put a roof o'er her an' keep her safe from the world outside. But there was nothin' I could do ta stop the pain o'what she saw in her visions. Yer stronger than her, thank God. The sight doesn't beat you down like it did her. Yer mam's nerves was frail an' she couldn't bear it after a while. She took to floatin' deliberate, so as to escape it.'

'Deliberate?' I sucked in my breath sharp.

'Aye. She'd float just ta spend time among the stars, she'd say.'

'Was that such a bad thing?' I asked, thinking of those nights recently when I'd done much the same. I lowered my lashes so as Da wouldn't see the guilt in my eyes.

Da sighed. 'There was one evenin' I came home an' you were bawlin' in the cradle. She was unconscious on the floor. Another time the place near went on fire an' she out cold in this chair. At night I became afeard to close me eyes in case she floated away in her sleep an' didn't come back.' His voice shook. 'An', one night, that's exactly what happened.'

'What d'you mean?' I was trembling and he took my hand.

'Yer mother left her body that night an' didn't return. I woke up an' she was gone.'

'That's how she died?'

He nodded. 'She'd left me an' you, of her own free will. In my heart I've tried to forgive her but I've never been able.'

'So what Mary Kate said is true: you do hate my mother.' I blurted the words out, half-choking on them, thinking as how he'd hate me an' all iffen he knew I too had learned how to float away at will. Iffen he knew how I danced above the chimneys and dreamed o' drifting up to the stars.

'No, no, lovey.' He lifted my chin and forced me to look him in the eye. 'I never hated yer mam but I came to hate her gift. I hated how the visions filled her mind till she could do nowt all day but shake an' cry. When she first started floatin' it seemed like a godsend because it gave her ease. But before long it took her over entirely. She was like one gin-addled; she cared about no one nor nothin' else.'

'No one?' I asked in a small voice.

'No one but you an' me. She wouldn't go outside, wouldn't talk to no one else, even to Missus Kenny or the sisters downstairs. When I'd go to work she'd lock herself in here with you. Two pretty birds in a cage, she'd say, shut safe away from the bad world. She'd croon an' sing to ya.' Da pulled me close. 'She'd be all right of a mornin', all bright an' cheery after her night flight, but when I'd come home o' an evenin' she'd be all broken again. She'd shove you into my arms an' crawl into the bed an' beg for sleep to come quick so she could escape the voices in her head. I knew it were wrong. I knew how it would end. With time she got sick o' my beggin' her to stop an' wouldn't listen to me no more. I swear you was all kept her here as long as she stayed.'

He tipped my chin up again. 'D'ya understand how terrified I was when I saw those same gifts comin' out in you?'

I nodded, chilled to the bone by what he'd told me. My mother's gifts had destroyed her because she'd not been strong-minded enough to control them. Or perhaps she'd never realised that she needed to master them?

'But you can't float like she could,' he said, smiling at me.

'I know it's happened you 'gainst yer will, but so long as you never seek it, you'll be safe. An' you won't seek it, sure you won't?'

'No, Da, I won't,' I promised. And inside I swore to myself that this time I'd keep my word.

Missus Kenny came rushing in the door with Mary Kate and Jon Jon behind her.

'What terrible news!' she exclaimed. 'That young Billy Bowl should ha' turned to such awful crime to feed his gamin' habits! An' Taney has ta leave us! What's the world come to? But you'll go to my sister in Bristol, my dear. She has a shop an' iffen she can't hire you, she'll find someone as will.' She handed me a piece of paper with a name and address wrote on it. 'An' you'll need a travellin' cloak for it isn't proper summer weather yet.' She had a red one in her arms. She shook it out and put it round my shoulders. 'There now, that's better.'

Hushed voices called up the stairs asking if they could come in and the Misses Davies appeared. Miss Ruth was trying not to cry.

'Missus Kenny told us you are leaving, Taney. We'll miss you so. Jon Jon will have to come calling on us now or we shall be too lonely.' Miss Evelyn pressed a parcel of biscuits and some coins into my hand, and kissed my cheek.

'You will take care, my dear? You will write?' she said.

I nodded as Mary Kate passed sleepy Jon Jon to me and

Da leaned down to pick up my things. I couldn't talk no more. I could only nod and try to smile, as they walked me down the stairs to the alley. Da and me were to set off to the quays right away. There'd surely be a ship leaving for Wales or England in the next few hours.

'We need ta go,' Da said. 'Before this mornin' brings any more bad tidin's.'

'Wait! Give me yer pocket knife, Milo,' Mary Kate said. He took it from his belt and opened a blade. She wiped it on her apron, took a lock of my hair in her hand and cut the end off with the knife.

'For Jon Jon,' she said. She took him outta my arms then and passed him to Missus Kenny. 'I'll not let him forget you,' she said. She took my face in her hands and it was all I could do not to break down and beg her to find a way, some way, that I could stay. 'Iffen you always try to do what you think is right, then you can't go far wrong,' she said.

I shook my head. 'That's what I thought I was doing, an' look at the mess I made.'

'You didn't make this happen, Taney. Billy had a hard life, God knows, but he chose to do what he done, an' no one else to blame but his self.'

I nodded, though I didn't really believe it. I kissed the Misses Davies, and Missus Kenny. The tears came flowing. That night, one way or t'other, I was saying goodbye to all the friends I'd ever had. I was leaving Thundercut Alley now, not knowing iffen I'd ever come back. I hugged Jon Jon and kissed his wee face. He wrapped his little arms tight around my neck and Mary Kate had to prise them offa me for I couldn't pull away.

Da and me didn't talk much on the way to the docks. He carried my bundle and I carried my locking box and he held my free hand like he used when I was a little girl. I swear he never left the quay that morning till my ship was outta sight and halfway 'cross the Irish Sea.

That first month in Bristol was a blur. Missus Kenny's sister, Agnes, runs a second-hand clothes shop an' all and she gave me a job tending it with her, though she already has an assistant name of Elsie. I have a bedroom in the attic, my own wee sky parlour with a view o'er chimney pots, not that I noticed the view much when I first arrived. I went about in a daze, my head always full of Billy and what he'd done, wondering what was happening to him now and would I never see him again. Wishing I could go back and change things, make everything right. But then I'd remember the girl he killed. There's no bringing her back. Her dreams are in the grave with her.

They didn't hang Billy. They never tried him for the Grange Gorman strangling seen as they'd no proof he done it and he never did confess. They hadn't the stomach for hanging a legless man, Missus Kenny suggested in a letter what came a few months back. They put him in Green Street gaol and he does what hard labour they can put him to. Even though he were only ever found guilty of that attack in Richardson's Lane, they say he'll never be let go free for fear he really is the Stoneybatter Strangler.

I never call him that in my mind. For me he's always Billy: Billy who taught me it's all right to be different, Billy who told me my gifts were special, who encouraged me to use them and learn how to control them. Billy, my best friend.

I wrote Mary Kate and asked her to go visit him and she said as there was no need, for he has become so famous that all sorts of folk tip the gaoler to catch sight of the notorious Billy-the-bowl and spend a half hour in his company. She heard a duke called on him just last week.

I'm mindful of my promise to Da. I don't float deliberate no more. There's been many a night I've looked outta my attic window, homesick and lonely despite all Agnes' kindness. The night has called to me in soft whispers.

'Come out, Taney Tyrell,' it says. 'Come out amongst the chimneys and dance with the stars.'

It takes all my strength not to go, for I know the joy of it, the weightlessness, the forgetfulness. I make myself think of my mother, and Billy too, how their need to escape pain only brought them misery. I don't blame them for what they did, not my mother, not Billy. I can't; I came close enough to going the same way. But I'll not be like them. There are other ways to find joy, to touch the sky. I have dreams of owning my own shop, my own home, someday. An' maybe I will, iffen I save the pennies I earn telling fortunes.

I still think of Billy all the time. Last night I dreamed we were up high, top of Kiss-arse-lane. Billy's rolling his bowl back a bit to get a good start. He's digging his batons into the ground and I've balled my fists set to run.

'Race ya!' he yells. 'Ready? One, two, three, go!'

He shoots off the top of the hill and sticks his batons under his oxters so as he can hold the sides of his bowl. I'm running so fast my legs are like windmills spinning in a storm. Billy's ahead of me, laughing an' yelling, and no matter how fast I run, I'll never catch him.

'Billeeeee!' I screech.

'Let go!' he shouts back o'er his shoulder. 'Fly, Taney Tyrell, fly!'

Acknowledgements

Many thanks to Padraigín Clancy for all her help with things Samhain; to Bernardine Nic Giolla Phádraig, the guides at Number Twenty Nine, Fitzwilliam Street, and the Jameson Distillery, Smithfield, for help with details; to Niamh White for reading and feedback; to Adele Griffin and Anna McCabe for providing emergency writing space.

Thanks to the folk at Clondalkin Library for going above and beyond to track down books for me; it's all in here somewhere!

As always, thanks to Jenny Glencross, my editor, and Eunice McMullen, my agent, for all the hard work and patience, and to my husband, Michael, for being my soundest of sounding boards.

Note: Billy was a real character of Georgian Dublin but I have taken liberties with his age.